CALCULATED RISK

By the same author

The Hills of Home
Love By Design

CALCULATED RISK

RAINBOW ROMANCE

PATRICIA McAUGHEY

Parkwest, New York
ROBERT HALE · LONDON

First published in the United States in 1993 by
Robert Hale/Parkwest Publications, New York

ISBN 07090-4919-6
Library of Congress Catalog Card Number 93-71969

First published in Great Britain 1993

ISBN 0 7090 4919 6

Robert Hale Limited
Clerkenwell House
Clerkenwell Green
London EC1R 0HT

Printed and bound by Interprint Ltd.,
Valletta, Malta.

One

"I'm sorry I'm late. I had an awful job finding somewhere to park." Catti flashed an apologetic smile at the woman who had come down the path to meet her. "I decided I'd leave the car in the village and walk up and that little car park was full and...." Her voice tailed off. Enough said! She certainly wasn't going to bother explaining that, as usual, the real reason for her being late was that she got carried away with a painting and had forgotten the time. This cool-eyed woman would never understand.

"How do you do. Miss Catherine Benson, isn't it?" She checked the name against the clipboard she was cuddling to her bosom and offered Catti a lightweight, professional smile. "You are *very* late, I'm afraid. We did say 11.30, didn't we?" She glanced at her watch and sighed. "This is going to play havoc with my appointments for the rest of the day."

"Is it?" If that remark was designed to make Catti feel guilty, it certainly succeeded. "What can I say? I've driven over from Chartscross as quickly as I could, but it still takes half an hour and the road was icy over the hill." She searched for some sympathy in the other woman's face but there was none.

Catti carried on regardless in the same cheerful vein. "Have you been in the village? There's a bus trip in, I think, and it's crammed with tourists. They're all jammed in the coffee shop trying to keep warm."

"Tourists!" She sniffed her contempt, adjusting large-framed spectacles. "One of the penalties, Miss Benson, of living in such a beautiful area. Serve them right if they get stuck on Cragtop on the way back. Still ... I suppose we mustn't complain." She struggled with the thinnest of smiles.

"No, we must not complain," Catti said firmly. "I like tourists," she told her, prepared and feeling in the mood for a full-blown argument if this woman chose to co-operate. She'd had it up to here with locals who shunned the very people who brought some life and colour into the community. And they also happened to buy a fair chunk of her paintings too.

She took a deep breath and tried to relax. All in all, she had had a difficult week and her temper was at simmering point. And now this snooty-faced woman, elegant in a navy business suit, was succeeding in making her feel like a tramp. She wished she had taken the trouble to change, but that would have made her even later, incurring this woman's wrath all the more. Who was she anyway? The estate agent's assistant, that's who, and surely it was Catti who was doing her the favour, not the other way around. She shot a defiant glance at the immaculate navy suit, still ruffled by the woman's attitude to tourists.

"Please don't misunderstand me, Miss Benson, I like them too," she now said hastily, too hastily, a flush appearing on her carefully made-up face. She was in her middle thirties, only a little older than Catti herself, but, beneath the business suit, there was an awkwardness that Catti had not expected.

Her next words confirmed this, spoken in a suddenly hesitant voice. "I'm not sure how we should go about this viewing," she began, looking round vaguely as if for inspiration. "Would you mind, Miss Benson, if I showed you and the gentleman round the property together to save a little time? It's not our usual practice but I'm running so late ... of course, if you'd rather we didn't...?"

"Gentleman? What gentleman?" Catti squinted into the winter sun, shielding her eyes as it appeared in its fragile splendour from behind a bank of morning clouds. "Is someone else interested?" she asked bluntly, aware even as she said it that it was a stupid question to ask of an estate agent. Damn! She had tried to give the impression over the phone that this house, Bay's End, was just one of several properties on her viewing list, no more or less important than any of the others.

"Oh yes, it's attracted a lot of interest." This time the smile was genuine and Catti didn't doubt that what she said was true. Wouldn't you just know it? After being on the market for the last year with hardly anyone casting a second glance at it, it was now suddenly and inexplicably popular. And it had taken her this last year to get her finances sorted out, so that she was now in a position to make an offer.

"Who is this gentleman?" She dropped the question lightly, trying for nonchalance, wanting to know what she was up against.

Miss Wilkes consulted her clipboard. "A Mr Adam Trent. He's from outside the area. I understand he's in hotel management. Or was ..." she added vaguely. "We sent him particulars of this...." She waved her hand towards the impressive stone house that stood slightly above them on its hill overlooking the bay. It enjoyed a commanding position, almost acting as a lighthouse on Bay Head. "Apparently, it will do nicely for what he has in mind."

"What does he have in mind?" Catti pondered out loud, softening what sounded like an impertinent question with a smile. "He's not planning to open a hotel, is he?" A niggle of doubt stabbed at her. She had not anticipated any problems. This time Bay's End was going to be hers. This time she was not going to let it slip through her fingers. And this time her plans were not so half-baked, for now she had the money to see it through and she was damned if she was going to allow someone to take it from her. "It's not big enough for a hotel surely?" she said now, helplessly, to an impassive Miss Wilkes. "Unless he's intending to turn it into a guest-house?"

"I really have no idea what his plans are," Miss Wilkes replied tartly. "We don't question clients' reasons for wanting to own a particular property." She screwed up her face and looked over Catti's shoulder. "He should be here in a few minutes," she said. "Unless he's late too."

Fuming quietly, Catti ignored the remark. She could read the question in the woman's eyes. What do you want, Catherine Benson, with a house like this? A bit large for a single woman. Unattached. She smiled into a sudden awkward silence. "I hope he's careful with the gate," she said flippantly. "Did you notice, it's almost off its hinges."

"Yes, I'm sorry about that. An oversight. It's a minor

detail and we'll get it fixed next week." She pushed at her spectacles, a gesture Catti was beginning to recognize as a nervous one. "Isn't the view simply superb?" she said, with a blatant change of subject. "This view alone will sell this house. Some people would give their all to wake up to a view like this."

Catti would. "It's fantastic....' she breathed, allowing herself to turn at last and look properly at it, half in fear that something would have changed. To her relief, nothing had. It was precisely as she remembered it, it was just as it was imprinted on her memory, it was the view she often dreamed about. A little over two years ago, she had stood at this very spot and looked at this same view, Joe at her side.

The far end of the terraced garden was just out of sight as it sloped towards the cliff, becoming an even steeper cliff path, a private track leading to the pebbly beach, pebbles strewn with seaweed and broken shells. She could be out of the house in seconds, taking a walk before breakfast, stepping across the pebbles to the mudflats by the water's edge. Hard, ridged sand hurting little feet. She smiled as a memory of childhood surfaced. The cold water lapping all around as she stood paddling, toes curling with pleasure, the shriek as a tiny crab scuttled past.

The bay was treacherous and had to be respected for its quicksands, its swirling currents, but for all that, it was to Catti the most beautiful place on earth. She gave a deep sigh of contentment as, down in the lane, a car drew to a halt, a door slammed and there was the sound of a man's brisk footsteps, followed immediately by a loud, colourful curse as the gate finally succumbed, falling away from its fragile bonds, crashing to the ground with an almighty thud.

"Oh Lord...." Miss Wilkes, her composure badly dented, flew down the path, high heels clattering. "Leave it, Mr Trent," she called in a most unbusiness-like voice. "Do please leave it."

Suppressing a smile, Catti waited. Well, well, how convenient! That should put him in a foul mood for a start and a man in a foul mood was much more likely to pick faults. And even she, who had been in love with this house for years, could see that there were faults. The outside was in desperate need of a coat of paint and the garden was a mess. As to the interior, she dreaded to think. She winced at what a tasteful conversion really meant. Those people who had beaten her to it last time had never loved the house as she loved it. It had become an enormous white elephant of a second home, standing empty for most of the winter, facing the fierce seas and icy swirling winds completely alone, cold and miserable. She would love it, clothe it, warm it, put colourful rugs on the wooden floors, heavy silk-lined curtains at the many windows.

She was not going to be put off. This time she only had herself to please, there was no Joe at her side, quietly complaining, insisting that he didn't know why she wanted to move, that they'd be better off where they were, living over the shop in Windermere.

Joe! It could still happen quite suddenly and take her by surprise. Sharp memories. Painful memories. Hastily, she pushed such thoughts aside as Miss Wilkes reappeared, escorting a man up the path, pausing dramatically at an appropriate point and giving him the benefit of the view across the bay, distant purplish hills rising up from its further shores.

Controlling her impatience, Catti waited. My, Miss Wilkes was certainly trying hard, sales talk flying in all directions. She hadn't been half as pushy with Catti, but maybe that was because she regarded her as a timewaster.

It must be something to do with her state of dress, for Catti had to admit that, in paint-stained jeans, trainers and an old comfortable sweater, she did look hard-pressed to have sufficient funds to be a genuine buyer. She frowned down at herself, brushing a bit of winter foliage that had stuck to her jeans. Be honest. She did look as if she might just stretch to buying a garden shed.

The man, tall and powerfully built, was on the contrary immaculately dressed in superb quality, black slim-fitting trousers and a weighty cream sweater. If he was surprised as Catti was introduced as another prospective buyer, he hid it well, gripping her hand firmly and smiling politely into her eyes. At his side, Miss Wilkes was red-faced and thoroughly flustered.

Catti stole a second glance at him. He had blue eyes of a most unusual hue that she instinctively matched to shades on her palette. He was, as her friend Penny would say if she was here, absolutely one hundred per cent gorgeous. Just in time, she stopped herself from launching into a long-winded account of why she looked so unbelievably casual. On top of everything else, she had had no time to fiddle with her hair and it was just scraped back into a ponytail.

She wished wistfully that she was looking smarter for him. What an unfortunate first impression. Her face would be shining, a bit pinched from the cold, and she had not bothered with make-up or perfume. In addition to that, he would doubtless dismiss her as no competition for the ownership of the house. If that was the case, handsome or not, Mr Adam Trent could think again.

"What would you like to do then?" Miss Wilkes clutched the clipboard tighter to her chest and smiled nervously.

They stared at her in surprise. She was, Catti decided, becoming less professional by the minute. She revised her initial thoughts, warming a little to the woman's inexperience. She was obviously new to the job and, quite frankly, not yet up to being let loose on clients.

As Mr Trent made no reply, taking his time about looking at the house, Catti deemed it her responsibility to take charge. "I think I probably speak for Mr Trent, too," she began briskly, attempting to draw herself up taller, "when I say that it might be better if we viewed the house separately." She looked at him for support and, to her surprise, found the faintest trace of amusement in his expression. Did that mean he had got over the business with the gate? Did it mean that, like her, he wanted this house so desperately that he was willing to overlook its failings?

"I agree," he said solemnly. "You show Miss Benson round first, Miss Wilkes, and I'll take a closer look at the garden."

"Ah ... the garden. I should explain about that," Miss Wilkes said quickly. "It is just a little out of shape. It just needs a few weeds pulling out here and there."

"A few weeds!" Catti threw back her head and laughed. "It needs a full-time gardener to get it sorted out. It used to be such a pretty garden," she explained to the now bemused man at her side. "You can see it from the beach, you see, and it was a blaze of colour in summer, all sorts of flowers tumbling down the terraces to the cliff. People used to stop and point it out." She sighed. "The owner would turn in his grave if he could see it now," she added quietly.

Miss Wilkes's look was pure venom. "Some people prefer to start from scratch," she said, pushing furiously at her spectacles. "It gives them more scope. Now ... would you like me to show you round the interior, Miss Benson?"

"Oh no, there's no need," Catti said cheerfully. "I'll show myself around if you don't mind that. I'm very familiar with it," she said, stopping herself from giving them a potted history of the place. Judging by Miss Wilkes's expression, that would not be appreciated at this moment. She felt their eyes on her as she made her way up the path to the front door. An excitement tugged at her as she opened the door and stepped over a few crisp leaves into the large square hall. She stopped and listened.

There was the silence of a house empty for some months. A chill that made her shiver and a smell that she remembered from long ago. It was sufficient to transport her back to the time she had stood here with Joe. His face had been as unyielding as granite and he had remained totally unmoved by her childlike enthusiasm. He had insisted that they were daft to think of moving here. They would be much better off staying in the flat, the flat that Catti hated.

She had told him angrily that she was fed up sharing her life with camping gear, canoes and the miscellany of equipment necessary for scaling mountains and shooting rapids. She was not prepared to share her life any longer with the shop stock that managed to overflow even into their bedroom.

She had been working on him and who knows? To be honest, they could not really afford it then but now ... now that the shop was sold and the rest of Joe's money had come to her, now she could afford it but at what cost? The loss of her husband, that's what!

She fingered the wedding-ring she wore on a chain round her neck. Taking it off her finger and reverting to her maiden name had been the only way she could cope.

Tears were threatening, damn them. She blinked them away. It was coming into the house again, it had caught at her heart more than she had anticipated. It would pass. Nowadays, sadness passed almost as soon as it came. People were right, well-meaning people like Penny; it was getting easier.

She concentrated on the house. It was, to her artist's eye, a disastrous hotchpotch of colour, a very mixed palette that made her shake her head with a little smile. Tasteful conversion, my eye, although she most certainly approved of the new galleried library and the kitchen with its French country feel. They had done nothing, thank goodness, with the room she had previously earmarked as her domain, her studio. From its windows lay fantastic views of bay on one side and on the other, the lower gentle stretches of Cragtop, the rocky hill that dominated the village. It was absolutely perfect.

Catti stood quietly in the centre of the room and closed her eyes, letting the very special atmosphere settle round her. It made her feel so creative, itching to start work at once on a canvas. A seascape. She saw that, living here, she might become very dependent on the sea and its changing moods.

She jolted herself out of her reverie, for she could hear voices in the adjoining room. Quickly, she glanced at the remainder of the downstairs, peeping and withdrawing at once from the vulgarity of the shell pink and gold-plated bathroom. Satisfied that she had seen all she needed to see, she slipped out of the house through a side entrance, almost skidding down the path to the broken gate and the lane, where a beautifully restored white sports car of uncertain years was parked.

Catti admired it fleetingly. It figured of course. He looked like he might own a car as classy as this, just as she looked, at the moment, as if she owned an old Mini.

An old Mini it might be but it was her pride and joy and she tended to think of cars as a means of transport. It did the job admirably even though she neglected it. Approaching it from the coast road, for she was never able to visit Bordersbay without a walk by the sea, it took a while to realize that she was boxed in. A large battered van had squeezed in behind her, far too close, and she had precious little room for manoeuvre.

Fuming at the wheel, she considered the possibility of extracting the little car from its trap. It could be done but it would take an awful lot of skilful toing and froing.

"Having trouble?" A car slid to a halt beside her, a white sports car, and Adam Trent smiled at her. "You'll never get it out of there."

"Want to bet?" she asked sweetly, winding the window down and smiling in return. "You're blocking the road," she pointed out, as an impatient horn sounded. "You'd better move on."

"Not until you agree to come and have a coffee with me. By the time you get back, somebody will have moved, so you'll save yourself a lot of trouble."

That was true. And, to be honest, she didn't really fancy her chances of getting the car out in one piece. "All right," she said ungraciously, "I suppose you're right. But I'm not sure, under the circumstances, if we ought to be meeting socially."

"Why ever not?" His surprise seemed genuine. He waved a hand in apology to the hooting driver behind. "I'll be right back," he said. "Don't go away."

She didn't have much option. Catti watched as he zoomed off, slotting his car expertly into a gap up ahead. Suddenly realizing that he would be back in a minute, her hands flew to her bag, whipping out lipstick and hair-brush. She dragged her hair from the narrow ribbon and fluffed it out so that it stood like a shocked red halo round her face. Wild hair. Hair very much with a mind of its own, she thought ruefully, trying to flatten it down a little. Checking her appearance in the car mirror, her brown eyes stared back, the sadness lurking there somewhere, and she hastily looked away as her fellow househunter appeared, swinging his car keys in his hand, waiting for her to emerge.

"You say where," he said, making no comment on what she hoped was a new, improved appearance but noting it none the less. She saw it in his eyes, a warm look, a flash of a glance that travelled like the speed of light but took her in from top to toe.

"We'll go to The Rendezvous," Catti suggested, trying her best not to look at him as she shepherded him through the busy little hilly street towards the cafe. She was acutely aware of him and already something about his face, his eyes, was worming its way into her subconscious. Memory was a funny thing, she reflected soberly, there were times now when she had trouble recalling details of Joe and she had not a single photograph to help her, as she had thrown them all away in one desperately unhappy moment shortly after he was killed.

They were shown to a table by the window in the smart little cafe. She liked The Rendezvous, with its lovely coffee smell, its pine furniture, its red-and-white checked tablecloths, tiny pots of fresh flowers on every table.

"Why shouldn't we have a coffee together?" he enquired lazily, when they had ordered. "I see no reason why we shouldn't."

"I do," Catti retorted. "After all, we are rivals." She eyed him with suspicion. "I hope this isn't a ploy, Mr Trent, to find out just *how* interested I am and whether I'm putting in an offer or not?"

"As if I'd stoop so low," he chuckled, smiling disturbingly right into her eyes and making her turn away quickly. "Incidentally, what are you offering?"

Her indignation bubbled over before she realized he was joking and a little reluctantly, she joined him in a smile. He was rather nice and it was such a pity that he should be the one man who might just spoil things for her. She had been so convinced that her offer would be snapped up that she had already been window shopping for the house. She had even ordered a bright yellow sofa that would look wonderful in the library.

Too many plans. A mistake. Now she was no longer sure she would get the house at all, for it all depended on this man. A man who had managed in a very short time to make quite an impression on her.

"I wouldn't dream of asking what you intend to offer," he continued, his smile vanishing as he stirred his coffee thoughtfully. "However, I do find myself a bit puzzled. According to Miss Wilkes you live alone. You paint, I understand? I ask myself, what does a talented, beautiful lady who lives alone want with a barn of a house like that?"

She noted the 'beautiful' and her heart soared, but she made no comment, choosing to go on the attack instead. "How dare that woman discuss me with you," she fumed, embarrassed as she caught the table with her sleeve and the cutlery jangled.

She rearranged it furiously, lowering her voice as a few people glanced their way. "What else did she tell you? That I illustrate children's books? That I paint seascapes when I get the chance and that I happen to live alone, yes, not from choice but because...." She stopped suddenly. "I'm sorry," she said, aware she might be accused of overreacting. "But it's a bit much, isn't it? Why I want the house is my business. It's nothing to do with anyone else."

"No, it isn't." He waved his hand in apology. "Point taken."

"After all, I'm not asking you why you want the house," she ploughed on, still ruffled, still not quite able to let the subject drop. "Although as you're in hotel management, it doesn't take much working out."

"Miss Wilkes told you that, I suppose? Discretion's

certainly not her strong point, is it?"

Catti exchanged a reluctant smile with him. "Are you really planning to make Bay's End a hotel if you get it?"

He smiled. "I thought you weren't asking why I wanted it," he reminded her. "Any plans I have are only at the provisional stage as yet."

"I see, Mr Trent."

"Oh ... please call me Adam. After all, we might be seeing a lot more of each other."

She hesitated a moment. "If you insist," she said quietly. "And I'm Catherine, Catti to my friends."

"Catti?" He smiled again. "Unusual and not entirely appropriate. I think I prefer Catherine...."

"As you like." She shrugged. It mattered neither way to her. She was becoming a little confused, not sure where this gentle sparring was leading. "Would you mind if we didn't discuss the house any more," she said with a sigh. "We ought to do that with the estate agent and no one else."

"You're right, of course." He smiled and it registered again that he was a very attractive man. Not that she was in any hurry to get involved with another man. Penny had tried time and time again. Well meaning, of course, but always unmitigated disasters. For the time being, she was perfectly happy as she was, kept very busy and fulfilled with her work.

"I'm sorry. I wasn't listening," she now confessed, as it dawned on her that he was looking expectantly at her.

"Me and my scintillating conversation," he said drily. "I was merely trying to lighten the mood. I was saying how lucky you are to live in such an unspoilt part of the country. And I also asked if you'd like another coffee."

"Oh no, thank you, I must get back." She considered the first part of his remark with a smile. "It is lovely round here, isn't it? I've never wanted to live anywhere else. Why have you decided to come here?"

"Because it's so unspoilt. You know, Catherine, when I was living abroad years ago, I dreamed of places like this."

"Where did you live?"

"Here and there. Kathmandu was my last base. More than ten years ago now...." He paused thoughtfully. "A long time. I decided it was time I came back and became a sober citizen. So ... that's what I did."

Kathmandu! Thinking about it much later, it ought to have struck a chord with her, an uncomfortable chord, but at the time it did not. She was so intent on watching him as he spoke, greedily drinking in his face, his eyes, his smile. Never before, not even with Joe, had she felt quite like this. Sitting opposite him, she found herself hoping that he had noticed her too, as a woman.

"How nice," she muttered inanely, masking her feelings with a bright smile. "Where are you staying while you look for a house?"

"I'm staying in a rented cottage about a couple of miles from Chartscross. It's up a track that says it's unfit for cars and by God, it's not lying. We manage to struggle up but when you get there, it's worth it. The view's really something."

"I live in Chartscross at the moment," Catti informed him, regaining some of her composure. She had just given herself a ticking-off. It must be the excitement of seeing the house again. It was making her act in this ridiculous way. Why, for goodness sake, she had only just met him.... "I used to live in Bordersbay as a child," she explained, pushing her empty coffee cup away. "I've been trying to move back here for years. I very nearly bought Bay's End when it was last on the market but I had to back out because my husband....." She stopped, automatically fingering the ring. "My husband's dead, Mr Trent."

His eyes were kind. He said nothing, fishing in his pocket and extracting a wallet. "Come on," he said. "Let's get you back and see if you can get your car out now."

She had no idea why she had told him about Joe. On such a short acquaintance? Fortunately, he chose not to press her about it, escorting her out of the cafe into a now quieter street.

It was cooler, thick dark clouds were gathering and there were a few spits of rain, cold rain, as they neared the car. The van had gone, leaving her free to do a simple reverse.

"Perhaps we'll meet again, Catherine?" He leaned over and smiled down into her face, one hand leisurely placed on the car window.

The engine spluttered into life. "One of us is going to be disappointed," she managed to say. "About the house...."

"May the best man win," he said, patting the window in a dismissive gesture. "No hard feelings, I hope?"

"No, of course not."

She could not help feeling a little sorry for him as she drove away. He would probably never speak to her again when she moved into the house. She would certainly never speak to him if he did.

So either way, the relationship, whatever it might have been, was irrevocably doomed.

It was a sobering thought and it stayed with her as she drove back through the gathering gloom, letting herself into her house which was on the prettier side of Chartscross.

On the kitchen table, a note was propped up. It was from Grace, her cleaning lady, to say that Penny had phoned twice. Oh dear! She tried to keep those two apart. Penny thought it an enormous extravagance for her to employ someone to do the housework, implying that Catti could do it well enough herself. Maybe, but, working from home as she did, she had to have some rules as it would be so easy to abandon work for the day and flutter around.

Penny could wait. Whatever she had to say would hardly be earth-shattering, and she needed a moment's rest to collect her thoughts together. What an extraordinary day! Damn Adam Trent. She had done nothing else since she met him but think about him, think about him in an irritatingly feminine way, think about him quite frankly in a way that completely foxed her. What on earth was the matter with her? Sex was something she could take or leave. That side of marriage had been a distinct disappointment with Joe. Joe always had his mind on other things.

The phone rang as she was carrying a tray through to the living-room. She snatched at the phone in passing, holding it awkwardly as Penny's cheerful voice exploded on her. "Where the hell have you been? I've been trying to reach you for ages and all I could get was Grace."

"I've only just got in. Hang on...." Catti put down the tray and plumped up the sofa cushions before sinking down. "I've been over to Bordersbay. Sorry I didn't call on you but I didn't have time. I've been looking at Bay's End." She volunteered the information before Penny should start quizzing her, as she was in no mood for a cat and mouse game.

"Have you honestly? Oh Catti ... I thought you'd got that place out of your system. It's far too big for you. I can't understand why you want to be bothered with a house that size."

"I told you that I was going to try for it as soon as the shop deal was settled," Catti told her, slightly irritated. "So I don't see why you're surprised. I'm going to put in my offer and then try to forget it for a while. She tucked her legs up underneath her, as Penny's chats could go on forever. "I've got to put all my energies now into getting these current illustrations finished."

"You will let the girls see them before you send them off, won't you? They tell all their friends that you draw pictures, you know?" She gave a short laugh before changing the subject in that abrupt way of hers. "What you need, Catti, is something to take your mind off things. It's high time I fixed you up with another man. That'd be a good diversion and it just so happens that...."

"Oh no you don't," Catti interrupted swiftly. "I am not coming to one of your get-togethers where, by the strangest coincidence, there happens to be an unattached male. I don't know where you drag them up from. Did I ever tell you about that last one? The one who was interested in photography?"

"Oh him," Penny dismissed it. "You're too fussy, that's your trouble. You'll never find the exact Mr Right, believe me. Take my Don, for example. Do you know what he's doing at this very moment? Sitting in front of the television waiting for Suzanne Roye's programme to come on and, when it does, he'll sit there starry-eyed for half an hour." She laughed with no trace of repentance as Catti heard Don's protest. "He sends his love by the way, Catti."

"Give him mine." Catti smiled into the phone. She liked Penny and Don. They were utterly devoted to each other and she took Penny's occasional manic grumblings with a huge pinch of salt. On an impulse, she found herself telling Penny about her meeting with Adam Trent. "He drives a sports car," she finished, hearing Penny whistle down the wire. "A white Morgan."

"Does he now? What will you do if he gets the house?"

A cold fear gripped her. "He won't, will he?"

"How should I know?" Penny said reasonably. "You sound as if you got that estate agent wound up, telling her the garden was a mess and everything."

"Houses are not bought and sold on that principle," Catti said stiffly. "The offers will be passed to the vendors and they'll make up their minds."

"Okay, don't get on your high horse, but, if I were you ..." there was the slightest pause, "I wouldn't build your hopes up too much. By the way, what does this Mr Trent look like?"

Catti gave a mock groan. "I wondered when that was coming. I can't even chat to the postman without you muttering about an engagement. He's so-so," she said, knowing full well the nonchalant tone would not fool Penny.

It didn't. "Is he indeed?" she drawled, humour not far from the surface of her voice. "Hey ... wait a minute, a white Morgan? It must be the fella who's renting Whichway Cottage. Bound to be him. There can't be that many white Morgans about."

"Do you know him?"

"I know of him. He goes into the little post office on Browbank and Helen says she's been fluttering her eyes for weeks to no avail. So-so – you liar, Catti."

"All right then, he does have a certain charm and I could see that some women might find him attractive," Catti said carefully. Her mind wandered a moment as she found herself recalling the blue of those eyes, the firm set of the jaw, that devastating smile, the gentle laugh, the way most of all that he looked at her.

"Are you there?" Penny's voice broke in. "Oh, I thought I'd lost you, you went very quiet. Look .... what I rang for is this," she continued, suddenly brisk. "I've lost Marjorie's services for the next week or so and, if anything should crop up this week-end, I'll be sunk. So I couldn't possibly call on you if I do need help? I mean there's a good chance that not a soul will contact me but in case they do...."

"Penny, stop it," Catti laughed, relaxed. "Of course I'll help. You don't even need to ask. I've no plans."

"You should have." Penny sounded relieved. "Thanks, that's marvellous of you."

"You're welcome. I don't want to be the cause of Penny Perfect Parties going under," Catti said. "How is business, Penny?"

"Not bad. I've got a silver wedding booked for next month, buffet for forty, and a couple of dinner parties for six as well, but nothing so far this week-end."

"There's time yet," Catti reassured her. "Hey ... what will you want me to do? You don't want me to do any cooking, do you?"

"I certainly do not. I have a reputation to keep up. You'll just be the general dogsbody."

"I see. Washing-up, I suppose?" Catti was still smiling as she replaced the receiver shortly afterwards, cradling the phone in her lap. She needed friends like Penny and Don, who were originally Joe's friends rather than hers for it was Joe and Don who shared a common interest.

Now why should she be reminded of that? In a sense, her attempt to buy Bay's End was to try and lay a ghost. Cragtop had been one of Joe's favourite short practice climbs, its rocky face difficult and exhilarating. And, from the rear of the house, she could see that very face. Sometimes, it was better to confront things head on. She felt sure now that she could cope.

Just one more climb. And to think she had believed that. One more climb and he was going to hang up his climbing boots and concentrate on the shop and being married to her. The mountains had been his first love and it was difficult to be second best. Catti had seen the obsession in his eyes when he talked about climbing, trying and failing to understand his motives. She had therefore been excluded from that important part of his life and that had been hard to bear.

With a sigh, she switched on the television and Suzanne Roye's beautiful ice-blonde image filled the screen. She was smiling in that slightly insidious way of hers at the poor unfortunate opposite her. Why on earth did people subject themselves to her interviewing technique? It brought humiliation at the very least. Catti found it impossible to watch without squirming.

Unable to relax, she switched off and flopped back onto the sofa. For some reason, she found herself thinking again about him. A warm feeling caught at her, as a sudden vision of him appeared. Trust him to be involved with the house; her competitor, her rival for its affection. She hoped he would look after it if he did get it.

A lump stuck in her throat as she considered that very real possibility. Surely not. Not after all her plans, it wasn't fair. She had waited so long for the right moment.

Damn him. And yet, there was no point in denying those little hot dizzy impulses she had felt when she was near him. Something had sparkled between them and she knew he felt it too. It had made it difficult to look him in the eye, for she was almost afraid of what she might see there.

Two

Adam Trent was nearly at his destination, having driven round the wide arc of the bay, when he allowed himself to recall the girl he had met at the house. Red-head. Funny, that – he didn't normally go for red-heads but she was different. Unusual face. Quite startling brown eyes and such cloudy hair the colour of warmth and promise. And, on top of all that, she had blushed. He smiled slightly. Blushing, it seemed to him, was a long-forgotten art. It went with smelling salts and maid-servants.

Pity they were off to a bad start. God knows what she would say when she found that he had already bought the house. Just the final document to sign and that was it. It was a stroke of luck that, just when he had been in the market for a house, an old friend, Harry Clarke, happened to be selling. A few private words, a hand-shake, and the matter was as good as settled.

It was a perfect location for his planned business venture. Big enough but not too big. He was looking forward to striking out on his own after years in the Tweed hotel chain. Assistant Manager here, Under Manager there, Manager, Regional Manager. Only a fool would give that up, particularly with promotion once more in the offing. Pension to look forward to eventually. Security.

But he was a climber at heart and just occasionally a climber took a risk, a calculated one, and this was one such risk. After ten years, it was time he did. Yes indeed, the last ten years had been an unqualified success for him.

Not quite. A sigh escaped him. His turbulent marriage had to count as a bad patch. He was determined not to repeat the mistake. One broken marriage could just about be tolerated but not two. He had enjoyed one or two romantic encounters since, but had backed away when the women had begun to look proprietorial.

Against the windscreen of the car, heavy rain lashed and the wipers were working hard to keep a clear screen. He concentrated for a while on his driving, aware he had been dreaming, peering at the roadsigns as he approached his mother's house. He still thought of the old house his mother lived in as home, probably because he had never had a proper home of his own, flitting about the country from top to bottom, living in company accommodation. And there had never been anyone to make it home. Suzanne had not been a homemaker.

He signalled to turn into the long drive that led to Belmont. There was no point in feeling sorry for himself. He was approaching a turning point in his life, dammit, and he ought to be excited and optimistic, certainly not dipping into self-pity, which he despised.

He thrust flowers at his mother, before she had the chance to remind him he was late. "The weather's foul, it's snowing over the high ground," he told her, kissing her powdered cheek and holding her close a moment. She smelled comfortingly of the eau-de-cologne she had always used. Pastelled and pearled as ever and pretty for a woman in her sixties.

"Go and get warm, I'll put these in water." She eyed them more closely. "How much did you pay for these, darling? They're past their best." She clicked her tongue. "I suppose they might just revive. It was a kind thought...." She smiled at him. "You're hopeless," she murmured fondly. "For a man who's expert at running hotels, you're not the least capable of running yourself. I bet you wouldn't stand for droopy flowers at a Tweed hotel."

Adam grinned, refusing to be ruffled. "They are pretty awful, aren't they?" he admitted. "Only thing I could get. There isn't a decent shop between Bordersbay and here. Not to worry, I'll run you into town later and buy you some more."

"You'll do no such thing." She bustled off in search of a vase. Adam wandered into the family sitting-room at the rear of the rambling old house. He stood a moment in the doorway, taking it in. It had changed so little over the years, still retaining the beloved old furniture, the lace mats, the clutter of ornaments his mother loved, family paraphernalia that always managed to bring a lump to his throat. What was it about returning to your childhood home that made you feel like a child again? With a little sigh for times past, he crossed to the big bay window, pulling back the faded velvet curtains to look out onto the big untidy garden.

That bare time of year. Poised, expectant for spring, his favourite time, when it would be aglow with daffodils.

He shivered, turning back into the warmth of the room where a log fire burned in the grate. His mother returned, the flowers tastefully arranged in a vase, waving towards him irritably. "Do sit down, darling," she said, "you're too large to hover. Now ... what have I to tell you?" she mused. "It's so long since I saw you." She raised her eyebrows, indicating her displeasure at that, but the twinkle in her blue eyes told him she did not really mind. "Oh yes, that's it. Suzanne rang. Sometime last week." She eyed him shrewdly. "She usually rings a couple of times a month. I think that's rather nice of her, don't you?"

Adam nodded. He had to concede that. For whatever reason, and he felt ashamed that he should consider there was an ulterior motive, Suzanne kept in touch with his mother. Hoping that she was not going to go on at length about it, as she was apt to do, he attempted a diversion, reaching for a slice of the chocolate cake he knew she had made specially for him. "Nobody can bake a cake like you," he said, smiling at her, as her face instantly lit up. He meant it. Baking a cake for someone, he thought philosophically, was an outpouring of love. It went without saying that Suzanne had never baked a cake for him. She was not a cake-baking woman. Who was nowadays? He recalled it had once been the cause of a major row. He remembered her lack of humour. Damn, he had only meant it as a joke. In truth, he couldn't care less but Suzanne had taken it to heart.

His mother was watching him intently. She was, he knew, about to launch into a lecture but was taking her time, picking up her knitting, something pink and fluffy, and consulting a pattern. "Of course I know it's quite hopeless with you two..." she began, her fingers moving effortlessly. "It was a sad day, Adam, when you and

Suzanne ... when you ..." she paused, apparently unable to bring herself to say the words.

Adam had no such qualms. "When we split up, you mean?" he said, making himself comfortable in the squashy old chair that had been his father's, stroking his hands over the fat chintz arms ... remembering. Was it his imagination or did a faint odour remain of the cigars his father had smoked? He looked directly at his mother, who had paused in mid-stitch. "It happens all the time," he said stiffly. "You know how high the divorce rate is, Mother."

"More's the pity," she said, tight-lipped, coming to the end of the row and expertly switching needles. "In my day, we didn't give in so easily. Every marriage has its rough moments but we fought through them. We took our vows seriously."

"Meaning I didn't ..." Adam sighed, brightening with an effort. "How about another piece of cake?"

She smiled slightly. "You're very good at changing the subject, Adam, you always were." She put the knitting aside, the needles perilously upright. "I told Suzanne, by the way, where you are. I never know whether you two are in communication or not. She does not mention you." She glanced towards him slyly. "I hope it wasn't meant to be a secret."

"No, it's no secret," he said easily. "In fact, she's coming up to see me next week-end."

"Is she?" Her hands flew to the pearls of her neck. "Oh ... that is nice."

"It's nothing like that." Adam was thoroughly disconcerted as he saw the hope in her eyes. "It isn't a reconciliation," he added, "our marriage is over. I don't suppose she told you but she's planning to get married again the spring. He's called Bruce. A producer I believe." He hesitated a moment, realizing he was not going to get away with as little as that. "She's moved into his house by the Thames. You should see it! I've met him. Seems a decent sort of bloke."

"How civilized!" She pursed her lips in evident disapproval. "No, she did not mention it because she knows I most certainly would not improve of that dubious arrangement." She smiled gently. "I'm so sorry, darling. Did you hope that one day...?"

"No I did not." He spoke firmly, finding himself clenching his fists in annoyance. When would she accept it was over? Their love could not be resuscitated. No hope of that.

Now, he found it difficult even to like her. The abrasiveness that had started as her gimmick on screen had rubbed off. All the gentle qualities had been erased and nothing could bring them back. A sudden vision of Catherine appeared. She oozed gentleness underneath that pretend bossy exterior. That was a sham he had seen right through.

It took a minute to realize his mother had asked a question. "Oh ... just business," he said. "We are civilized people and we're not at daggers drawn. You know she's always been interested in the hotel business. She's coming up to discuss things as she's interested in putting up a financial share."

"Is that wise, dear? Won't she get under your feet?" She shook her head sadly. "I suppose you know what you're doing. Climbing holidays, isn't it? I couldn't imagine going on a holiday like that, being marched from pillar to post, ending up exhausted." She eyed him suspiciously. "Don't tell me Suzanne's suddenly developed an interest in that? She never made any effort to understand it when you were married, did she? She never gave you the slightest encouragement. Too busy, I suspect, deciding which nail polish went with which outfit."

Adam laughed, rather surprised by the ferocity of the attack. "You never liked her, did you? My God, you kept that well hidden." He gave a small smile as her silence and busy burrowing in the knitting bag confirmed his words. "Perhaps that's why I'll probably not marry again," he muttered almost to himself. "It takes a very special woman to understand."

"Talking of climbing..." she murmured. "A little bird tells me there's a climb in the offing. Summer, isn't it?"

"Who told you that? Things aren't settled yet." He offered a reassuring smile. "It's ages nice I've had a proper climb. I'm going stale. And Stuart's organizing it so that should set your mind at rest."

"Stuart Patterson?" His mother visibly relaxed. "That's all right then, capable man. Will you go, darling?"

He took his time about replying, realizing he had been putting off the decision. "I'll only be there in a support role," he said slowly. "Too rusty for anything else. All I'll be doing is helping lug the equipment. More or less." His attention was caught by a movement outside the window as a bird flew past. "Of course, if he offers me the chance to do a bit of climbing, I'll take it. It nags at you after a while. I need to get back up there."

"So you're going." She made no comment. "Am I allowed to tell anyone or is it a deadly secret? What is the name of this mountain you will be ascending?"

Adam smiled at the phrase. "Well, it's certainly not Everest," he told her with a quick grin. "That's booked up for months ahead."

His sarcasm was rewarded with a look that made him feel about twelve years old again. "Everest or not," she said. "Make sure you don't fall off it."

The car was piled high with parcels, various things to make life at the cottage a little more palatable. Pretty bed-linen for the guest-room Suzanne would occupy this coming week-end. She had made that perfectly clear, as if it needed to be made clear. He had felt mildly insulted. He was fully in control of his feelings where Suzanne was concerned. She need have no worries that he intended to try to charm her back into his bed over the week-end.

He dumped the parcels in the hall and poured himself a drink, slumping in a chair in front of the spluttering gas fire. Suzanne expected opposition to his plans. "Bound to be trouble, sweetie," she had said in their last telephone conversation. "Bound to be. People hate change, particularly country folk." He could hear the sound of paper rustling. "Look, where is this place?" she asked. "We can't find it marked on the map."

"I'm not surprised. Try Chartscross, a few miles inland." Adam was amused as the paper-crackles and curses continued. "Found it? Now that's a proper town. It's even got a couple of department stores."

Her shrill laugh tinkled. "Really? I don't want to be a wet blanket, sweetie, but I always think the worst of people. I want this to succeed as much as you do. I've got money in it and I'm deadly serious about money. But people who live in little villages have such a narrow outlook on life. They'd still be driving round in horse-drawn carts if they'd had their way."

And so it had gone on and on. She had ended, to his annoyance, by practically dismissing the locals, as she insisted on calling them, as being a little problem he could safely leave to her. They would be utterly overwhelmed by her, she told him, they would call her "that woman on the telly" in hushed tones, they would fall over themselves to please her. In return, she would offer a couple of her old sweaters to auction for the church funds. Leave them to me, sweetie, and they'll agree to anything.

Workwise, she was terrifically excited. She was branching out, taking the show on location. No more cosy studio sets.

"I see. You mean you'll be interviewing a climber, for instance, halfway up the Eiger, roped to him...."

"Not quite." A chill had fluttered down the line. "Bruce says I should come to see you at your hovel," she had continued calmly. "No funny business, sweetie." Adam made no comment, his hand tightening on the phone as he controlled his anger. "I'll have to go," she said. "By the way, don't go to any trouble for little old me. Caviar and chips will do fine."

Caviar and chips indeed! Was he making a mistake in becoming involved again with Suzanne? It would mean he was partly bound to her once more, not by love, but for cold calculating business reasons. A mistake? Maybe ... time would tell. He could handle Suzanne.

He ran a hand through his hair, yawning hugely. He wished he was entertaining Catherine to dinner instead. He could just see her sitting across the table, that lovely hair fluffed around her gentle face. Gazing at him with those wonderful brown eyes. Somewhere, there were the first stirrings of desire. He sighed and pushed such thoughts aside. One thing at a time, and the most pressing difficulty was getting something organized for this week-end.

Wasn't there someone who advertised in the local paper? Someone who would do the lot? Simple fare probably but Suzanne might appreciate that after the nouvelle cuisine she was used to.

He flicked impatiently through the paper before he found it. There it was. Penny Perfect Parties and a telephone number.

He reached for the phone.

Three

Catti's Mini bumped and rocked its way up the track to Whichway Cottage. The nearer she got, the more she regretted her decision to help Penny out. Of all the people in Chartscross, he alone had to decide to have a dinner party this week-end, although, of course, he could not have known that she would be involved. It was all very well Penny insisting that he would not actually be there and that they would be long gone by the time he did arrive with his guest, it was still a worry.

To cap it all, Penny had never stopped talking about him, skimming the latest titbits from Helen by the ladelful, repeating it gleefully. Catti had feigned disinterest, deciding she was going to take a long time to forgive him ... if ever. She could certainly have done without this; helping to make sure his cosy tête à tête dinner was a big success. If she had her way, she would have laced his drink with arsenic.

He had bought Bay's End. Catti could still feel the numbing shock as Miss Wilkes, supposedly sympathetic, had explained that his offer had been accepted by the vendors. Disturbingly, Catti gained the impression that it had been cut and dried even before they viewed the property, even before he took her for a coffee, even before he managed to charm his way into her heart.

She was only doing this today for Penny. If he dared

show his face, she had warned Penny that she might very well do something to blacken the name of Perfect Parties forever. Smiling grimly at just what form that might take, Catti parked her Mini on a patch of rough ground beside Penny's estate car and jumped out, smelling the crisp clear air. The bay stretched grey and murky in the distance, the sea at one with the heavy sky, the horizon blurred.

Catti shivered, pulling her jacket closer and hurrying towards the cottage. She remembered visiting it as a child and thinking it a fairytale cottage, so remote and lonely, faintly disturbing in that way of some fairytales. It was further round the headland from Bordersbay on higher, craggier ground.

Rented out as a holiday let, it looked a touch forlorn, verging on the neglected, and Catti approached the door cautiously, half-expecting him to appear even though there was no sign of his sports car.

"Come on in, the door's off the latch," Penny called. "Give it a push, it sticks."

Catti almost fell into the dark hall, smiling at Penny who was in the kitchen doorway brandishing a fearsome looking knife. "Wait until you see this kitchen," she said. "It's the absolute pits." She squeezed over so that Catti could get by. "Small, eh?" Side-stepping to the sink, she continued chopping vegetables with aplomb, sliding them into a large earthenware pot. "That's the trouble with this job," she grumbled. "When clients want you to cook in their kitchen, it's either *Homes & Garden* stuff or like this." She sliced the air dangerously with the knife seeming to notice Catti for the first time. "I thought you were going to wear something pretty," she remarked, frowning down at Catti's casual attire.

"Why?" Catti asked aggressively. "I told you, Penny, I refuse to wear a cocktail dress and high heels just on the off-chance that Mr Trent will turn up. Especially as I am not the remotest bit interested in what he thinks about me."

"Aren't you?" Polly grinned maddeningly. "If you say so. By the say, I met him yesterday when he popped by to finalize arrangements and give me a key. You never hinted that he was quite so charming." She rolled her eyes. "Wow! He was amazed at the menu I suggested. He seemed to think all I could do was nursery teas."

"What do you want me to do first?" Catti whipped off her jacket, anxious to get Penny off this thorny subject. She did not wish to be reminded that Mr Trent was courteous, charming and good-looking. She knew it. Oh, how she knew it. She felt her heart constrict as she remembered just how much. "Shall I make us some coffee?" she volunteered, reaching for mugs.

"Wonderful idea." Thankfully, Penny was not pursuing the subject. "Would you take a look at his china," she said instead. "It all matches."

"You sound surprised."

"I am surprised. That's definitely a plus point for him," she added slyly. "Shows sensitivity. He must have known how I hate working with odds and ends. That's one of the things that irritates me about Don. He hasn't a clue about the finer points of life. It's all the climbing he used to do, of course."

Catti paid great attention to the coffee. "I don't see the connection," she muttered.

"Isn't it obvious? When they're up a mountain, the finer points of life have to fly out of the window. They eat off tin plates."

She was such a picture of indignation that Catti could not stop herself from laughing. "Of course they do," she said. "What else?"

Penny smiled too, cupping her hands round her coffee. "It's good to hear you laugh," she said. "It's just not worth getting yourself into such a tizzy about a house. And it really was too big for you, Catti. You'd have rattled around in it like a pea in a drum."

"I had other plans." Catti's brief attempt at cheerfulness subsided gently and she might have confided her plans but Penny became suddenly brisk, issuing orders at a trot if they were to be ready in time. Thus dismissed, Catti wandered into the little dining-room and set about preparing the table. Of all the rooms in the cottage, this was the nicest. The table was heavily dark and solid, the chairs high-backed and intricate, the sideboard rather splendid. A pale primrose, gently flowered wallpaper lightened the room and a couple of huge vases of dried autumn flowers made it very nearly pretty.

Catti found herself drawn to the window and the view of the bay. It was different from this angle, its wide perimeter obscured by the dense trees of the coast wood, which lent extra texture and movement even though the trees were bare of leaves. Catti's artist's eyes fully approved. Leaves and twigs underfoot. The smell of the salty sea. Seagulls wheeling above. Rustles in the undergrowth but nothing to be seen. A childhood paradise, a pot-pourri of scents and memories as vivid now as then.

"Hey ... stop dreaming and get on with it," Penny said bossily from behind. "We haven't much time. I want everything ready when they get here. Now ... let's see..." She checked the items on her fingers. "Starter in the fridge. Main course on automatic timer in the oven. Sweet also in the fridge. Cheese already out. Wine chilling. He'll have to do the coffee himself," she added, chewing worriedly on her lip.

"He's not completely helpless, is he?" Catti said with a sniff of irritation. "And he'll have his lady friend to help out. Surely she can manage to make some coffee and hand him a mint."

"I expect so." Penny was trying hard not to laugh. "We're not the teeniest bit jealous, are we?"

"I'm not, you might be," Catti replied tartly. "I just hope they appreciate all the trouble we've gone to."

They worked a moment in silence, covering the table with a pale blue linen cloth and laying out crystal and silver. "I would have preferred to stay and serve it," Penny said thoughtfully, standing back to admire the finished result. "But he wouldn't hear of it." She glanced knowingly at Catti. "You can guess why. A romantic candlelit dinner for two does not include a couple of ladies hovering in the kitchen. It might very well cramp his style and you never know what they might want to get up to afterwards."

"That's none of our business." Catti fussed a moment with the cutlery, suddenly finding herself asking if the lady was staying the week-end.

"How do I know?" Penny pretended to be shocked, her eyes betraying her. "Mind you, the guest bedroom's made up. Very pretty. Yellow and white. His room's at the front."

"You've been snooping. Penny, I'm surprised at you." Catti smiled as Penny had the grace to look ashamed.

"I was just looking. Awful wasn't it?" She frowned towards the centrepiece of real blooms. "Cut the stems a bit, would you? They're just a fraction too tall and we want them to be able to gaze into each other's eyes without restrictions, don't we?"

Catti was not sure she did. She felt like making it as difficult as possible for Adam Trent and his guest and the feeling puzzled and confused her. Why couldn't she get him out of her mind? Why was she starting to attach such a rosy glow to all thoughts of him? He had treated her shabbily, and what she saw as his underhanded approach about the house annoyed her intensely. He had allowed her to think there was some hope, that it was a straight fair fight.

Why then did she find herself sitting smiling at the thought of him? It was ridiculous and, despite her protestations to Penny, she *was* insanely jealous of this other woman in his life, this woman whom he would shortly be entertaining to dinner. This woman who was probably waiting even now at the station in Chartscross for him to....

The door opened and Adam Trent appeared, tossing newspapers onto the nearest chair. "I thought it was your car," he said with a slight frown. "What the hell are you doing here and where's Penny?"

"Penny's in the kitchen. I'm just helping her." Catti returned his frown, tossing her hair and staring at him. "We didn't expect you back," she said. "We understood you were picking up your friend from the station."

"Change of plan." He slipped his tan suede jacket off his shoulders and put it casually across the chair. He was wearing a dark green silk shirt, a shirt of beautiful quality with an embellishment of hand-stitching, tucked into black trousers. "She's driving up," he said, his voice husky, the slightest of smiles breaking forth. "She's bought a Bentley and she wants to try it out on a long drive."

"She'll ruin the suspension on the track."

He shrugged. "That's her problem." He ran a hand through his hair. "I'm sorry, you took me by surprise," he said. "You're the last person I expected to see."

"Or wanted to see," she said tersely. "Don't you think you owe me an explanation?"

"What for?" Again that innocent look in those blissful blue eyes. "You seem very uptight."

"I have every reason," she told him fiercely. "I'm a very busy woman, Mr Trent, and I do not like to waste my time."

"Hold on...." He held up a hand warningly. "Let's start again. For some reason, you seem to be in a foul mood."

"Correct in one. How very perceptive of you."

"Sarcasm too." A smile curled round his lips. "If this is about what I think it's about then I don't see that any explanation is necessary."

"Oh, but I do. I was told by Miss Wilkes, more or less, that your offer had already been accepted before you viewed the house that day with me."

"Indeed? You were told by Miss Wilkes?" He sank onto the chair but Catti remained standing. She was not going to make the mistake of relaxing in his presence.

"That woman is becoming something of a thorn in my flesh. Look Catherine ... let's just forget it, shall we?" he smiled easily, much too easily.

"We will certainly not forget it," she said, aware her voice was rising and powerless to prevent it. "I wanted that house very badly, Mr Trent." She regretted saying it but it was too late. It was said. It made her sound like a spoilt child, throwing a tantrum because she couldn't have what she wanted.

"I know you did," he said softly. "However ... I thought you and I had a gentleman's agreement?"

"I'm no gentleman," Catti hissed through clenched teeth, her whole body stiff and unyielding.

There was a silence. "Oh, I can see that," he said at last, quietly, catching his breath, and there could be no mistaking his meaning as his gaze travelled languidly from top to toe, taking in every inch.

Catti felt the blood rush to her face. It was a long, long time since a man had looked at her in quite that way and she had forgotten how pleasant it could be. Dammit, she was reacting in precisely the way she did not wish to react. Holding her head high, jutting out her breasts, arranging herself, albeit subconsciously, in a more seductive pose. Damn him! She knew she wanted him to touch her and kiss her. She had always felt herself shy with men, even Joe, so why should this man be so different? She didn't even know him. And, not only that, he had acted most dubiously where Bay's End was concerned.

He dropped his gaze first. "I'm sorry," he said roughly, "I'm sorry that you were so disappointed but I'm afraid business is business. I'm sure you'd be the first to agree with me on that and we shouldn't let our feelings get in the way of such things."

"It's easy for you to say," Catti said, taking a deep steadying breath. "You've got the house. I know I'm being a very bad sport but I can't help it. And don't expect me to offer my congratulations either."

"I don't expect that." A smile flitted over his face as he tried in vain to elicit a warmer response from her.

"I must get on. Penny will kill me if she finds I've not done these flowers yet."

"Oh yes, Penny. Formidable lady, isn't she? Leave the flowers," he said impatiently. "We can do without flowers. You wouldn't like to be an angel and make me a cup of tea, would you? Bring in an extra cup. You may as well join me if you can bear to sup with the opposition."

Catti was momentarily lost for words. Be an angel! Just who did he think he was? "I may join you in a cup of tea, Mr Trent," she said, with what she hoped was some semblance of dignity. "Although we are very busy at the moment preparing your meal for you and your *guest*." She didn't mean to stress the "guest" but stress it she did, and it caused a flicker of amusement to cross his face.

"Mr Trent? What's happened to Adam?" he asked softly. "You really wanted that house, Catherine, didn't you? If I'd have known how much...."

"You'd have backed off and let my offer stand?" she asked brightly. "Oh come on Adam, you've said business is business, so don't patronize me by pretending otherwise."

"Ouch!" He reeled back, a grimace on his face. "Hell

hath no fury like a woman deprived of the house she wanted."

For two pins, she could have slapped him across the face for that. But she did not, for, even as she thought it, she was fighting against a delicious warmth seeping through her, through her veins, fast dissolving the ice-cold anger.

"He's back already," she said to Penny as soon as she was in the kitchen. "So much for you saying he was meeting her at the station. She's driving up apparently. In a Bentley."

Penny raised her eyebrows. "She must have a bit of spare cash." She glanced at Catti with a faint smile. "You look flushed. Why on earth don't you try to relax? Forget the damned house and stop being so bitchy with him."

"You know what he said? 'Be an angel'."

Penny grinned. "Too true. He knows better than that. I'm sure it was just a slip of the tongue. He didn't mean to sound such an arrogant, insensitive, chauvinist pig."

"Have you been listening in?" Catti asked suspiciously, as she saw the teacups and the pot on the tray. "How could you?"

"You weren't exactly whispering." Penny passed over the tray. "Am I really formidable?"

"You do tend to boss people around but I don't think we mind particularly." Catti held the tray uncertainly. "Do you think I should go back in there?"

"Of course. Get in there before she arrives, whoever she is. You've got half an hour at most to bowl him over." She shook her head sadly. "I told you to wear something a bit more glam. He's only ever seen you in jeans."

"For goodness sake...." Catti lowered her voice, pulling a face at a totally unrepentant Penny. "You're always like this when there's a man in the offing. Any man. Anyone would think I was desperate. I've told you I'm very busy with my work and I'm perfectly happy as I am. To be honest, a man would just get in the way."

"You don't have to convince me. I'm sorry, Catti, I was just having a bit of fun. Just trying to cheer you up, that's all. I know you're not remotely serious about him."

Wasn't she? She checked her appearance in the hall mirror before taking the tray through. Pity about the jeans and sweater. At least her hair was looking good today, freshly washed and fluffed out, tumbling around her shoulders, golden glints amongst the fire of red.

He was standing at the window looking out onto the frosty twilight. It crossed Catti's mind briefly that she needed to get home over the moor before the roads became really icy. She put the tray down, standing awkwardly, not sure if she should disturb him. It seemed a discreet cough was called for and, sure enough, it was enough to make him spin round.

"Oh, thanks. No, do stay, I meant that. I want to make up for the bad start we've had. Here ... you sit down, let me pour the tea." He moved fast and she did as he asked, perched on the chair, accepting a cup of tea with a smile. "Now, Catherine ..." he said as he took a seat opposite. "Let's talk."

"About what?" she asked in some consternation. "I can't think of a single thing we have in common."

"There's the house," he said ruefully. "Sorry. At least

it's a start." He saw the look on her face and went on hurriedly. "Look, let's forget that for the moment. I've been thinking about what you said, Catherine, and I'd like to see some of your work someday. Your paintings."

"Would you?" He had this knack, this disturbing knack, of making her anger seem less pronounced. She struggled for some sense, some grace, as she felt suddenly and inexplicably shy.

"I'd be happy to show you," she said quietly. "I'm doing an exhibition of my work next summer, so perhaps you'd like to go along to that."

"I had hoped for a more personal viewing," he said. "If you've forgiven me yet of course...?"

She could not quite bring herself to say that. Not yet. But her feelings were so mixed where he was concerned that she was finding it increasingly difficult to keep her eyes off him. She was greedy for that gently caressing voice, soothed and lulled by it. What was it about him, about this man, that made her suddenly long to be held in his arms? She had thought, since Joe, that she had succeeded in relegating that part of life to being less important.

Until now. Until this lithe, dark-haired man with such blue eyes who looked at her as if he knew exactly what she was thinking. "I'd like to ask a favour of you," he said now. "I realize it's a little presumptuous of me after the way you feel I've treated you but...."

"What do you want?" she asked uncomfortably. "I hardly think that I can be much help."

"I want you to act as my guide round this area. I need to get to know it like the back of my hand. I know it vaguely, of course, in passing, but I want to get to know all the off the beaten track places."

"Can't you find out from tourist information?" she asked tartly, playing for time whilst she considered what to do.

"Yes, I suppose so," he said with a wry grin. "But I'd rather find out from you. Sometime next week perhaps after my visitor's gone?"

Did he have to remind her of that? It was oddly painful to think that he had a relationship with another woman, a woman whom she just knew would be beautiful. And apparently rich. How could she compete with that?

"I am busy," she demurred, although it wasn't true any more. The commission was complete and she could afford a little relaxation. "All right, I'll think up an itinerary," she said, with the slightest of smiles. "I'll take you to one of my favourite places, a little village beside a lake that not many people know about. Joe and I...." She stopped, seeing that she had to offer some explanation. "Joe was my husband," she said. "I told you ... he was killed in an accident about two years ago."

He happened to be beside her, having risen to his feet, and the reaching out and touching her shoulder was a nice gesture, a gesture of sympathy which she accepted silently. Not too long ago, that sort of thing would have brought tears to her eyes.

"Suzanne's just coming up on business," he said lightly, surprising her with the remark, coming out of the blue as it did. "That's all. She eats constantly in hotels and restaurants so it seemed a nice idea to do this. She'll probably think it quaint."

She wondered why he felt it necessary to explain. True or not, it was comforting that she was just a business associate. Funny how he just called her Suzanne as if Catti should know whom he was talking about. Awkward now, she struggled for something to say. Anything. She was achingly aware of his closeness and she knew he was of hers. It was a very powerful feeling that transmitted easily the short distance that separated them. Thankfully, the chiming of the clock jolted her out of her daze and she jumped up. "I must go," she said. "Penny will wonder what's going on."

"Of course." His hand brushed hers as he handed her the cup. Deliberate or not, she could not be sure. What she was sure of was her reaction. It was as if fire suddenly danced in her veins, scorchingly running through her, lighting up every far corner of her and she could not help a tremble.

"Don't be frightened of me, Catherine," he said softly, reaching towards her, holding her chin and tilting up her face so that she had no option but to look at him.

"I'm not." She laughed shakily. "Whatever gave you that idea?"

"Frightened of yourself then?"

"What do you mean?" She slipped his tender grasp and fussed with the tray, heart thumping.

"Are you always so nervous of men?"

"I'm not in the least nervous," she said, sorry her voice carried no conviction. "If you'll excuse me...."

He moved away, watching her with amusement as she passed. If only blushes could be controlled, she thought angrily, as she felt her cheeks flame. It was being a red-head, of course, her pale skin did tend to colour easily. "I'll call you," he said as he opened the door for her. "About our little trip."

"Oh yes," she called back, as casually as she was able. "I'm in the book."

"Well?" Penny pounced on her. "What did he say? Did he tell you anything about this woman who's coming to dinner?"

"Only that she's called Suzanne and she's a business associate."

"Is she now?" Penny looked as if she was going to challenge that but the sound of a car in the lane silenced her. A little guiltily, they peered out of the window into the dusk as a car's lights were dimmed.

A large car with a woman at the wheel. She stepped out, taking her time, slamming the door and waiting. She wore an ankle-length cream leather coat and her hair was tucked under a large fur hat. Adam was already striding out to meet her, giving her a peck on the cheek and a quick hug.

Penny dropped the curtain. "Good Lord," she said. "Was that...?"

Catti frowned. "Unless it's a look-alike...?"

"Like hell." Penny gave an expressive sniff. "Well I never! Just wait until I tell Don. He'll be around hotfoot for an autograph I shouldn't wonder."

"Do you think you should tell him?" Catti asked. "Suppose Adam doesn't want it to be generally known?"

"We haven't signed the Official Secrets Act," Penny said, exasperation showing. "How can he keep her secret for long? You know what the jungle drums are like round here." She whipped off her apron. "I think we'd better make ourselves scarce," she said. "Everything's ready. I hope they enjoy it."

"He said she was a business associate," Catti repeated, looking to Penny for reassurance. "You don't think that they're ... well...?"

"If she's just a business associate, I'll eat my hat," Penny said firmly, oblivious to Catti's reaction which verged on shock. "It's quite obvious they're lovers. Can't you tell?"

"Well, we suspected as much, didn't we?" Catti was overwhelmed by disappointment, trying desperately to hide it. Her senses were bruised, hurt. From the hall came the sound of voices, laughter, a woman's voice, an unmistakeable woman's voice, calling him "sweetie".

Catti slipped on her jacket. Soon, Suzanne Roye would be sitting opposite Adam, receiving the full nerve tingling jolt of that blue gaze. She thought again of the seductive note in his voice when he had whispered her name. Catherine ... no one had called her that for years, not even Joe. She felt a tightness descend on her. He had set out to charm her, to win her round after the fiasco with Bay's End, to toss an invitation her way he obviously had no intention of pursuing.

And like a little sentimental fool, she had fallen for it.

Four

Catti eased herself into the bath, settling amongst the scented bubbles with a sigh. A brief memory of the opulence of the bathrooms at Bay's End surfaced but she pushed that aside at once. Forget all that. She was refusing to dwell on what might have been. She would do what she had done with memories of Joe. Slip them into a compartment of her mind, take them out from time to time, dust them down, then return them.

Professionally, things were looking good. Her illustrations had been favourably received and more work was on its way. A new author had seen her portfolio, liked it and requested that she do the artwork for his children's book. With a light smile, Catti reflected that success or near success was a tricky phenomenon. It had a snowball effect and, if it continued like this then she might soon be in the marvellous position of picking and choosing her commissions. Oh, the delight of that.

She was just considering the pleasant dilemma when the phone rang. Damn! She'd never been able to leave a ringing phone, so, wrapping herself in a soft bathsheet, she padded down to answer it. Who could it be? Not Penny, because Penny knew better than to disturb her tonight, as this was her night for doing her nails, a pedicure and a face pack. The works!

She picked it up. "Catti Benson," she said, slightly

cross, wiping water off her face as it trickled down from wet ringlets of hair.

"Hello, Catherine. This is Adam Trent. How are you?"

She very nearly dropped the receiver. Her hand felt clammy, not quite in control. Penny was right. Over the phone, where every nuance of a voice could be heard, his was incredibly sexy, warm and wonderful. "I wasn't expecting you to call," she said, hitching up the towel as it threatened to slide seductively down her body.

"Yes you were," he argued pleasantly. "I thought we'd arranged that I should ring you."

"Yes I know but...." She didn't bother to explain that she had come to the conclusion that he wouldn't ring, that he would have forgotten her existence now that Suzanne Roye had appeared on the scene. "What is it?" she asked briskly. "You've got me out of the bath."

"Oh ... I'm sorry. Shall I ring back in ten minutes or so?"

"No, but can you be quick? It's chilly."

"Are you free tomorrow? I know it's short notice but I've been up to my eyes in various things. I thought we might take that drive round that you promised. We can stop off for lunch somewhere."

"That sounds lovely," she murmured. "What time?"

"Ten-ish? That all right? If you tell me exactly how to get to your house, I'll pick you up."

"The forecast's not too good," she said doubtfully. "We've got to get over a high pass that seems to get blocked if more than three snowflakes fall on it."

He laughed. "Sounds dreadful. Don't worry, we won't set out if there's the slightest danger of a snowstorm."

She could not help a little flutter of anticipatory excitement as she replaced the receiver. Catching sight of her reflection, she was not surprised to see a self-satisfied smile and a happily glowing face. Clutching the towel against her, she shot up the stairs to resume her bath.

The temperature had dropped sharply by next day and it promised to be clear and bright. One of those crisp, cold winter days when it was far better to be out in the open air than huddled over a fire.

What should she wear? This was the first occasion when she had the chance to wear something that he might like. But what? With an anxious glance at the clock, Catti surveyed the various items spread on the bed. She had started off as she meant to go on, wearing her best underwear, oyster silk and lace. Her hair was tousled from the effort of trying on and discarding a selection of outfits already. Her brand new emerald green suit with the longer skirt? It would look super with boots but ... they might be tramping about in the remains of last week's snow and wellies might be more appropriate. How about her oldish but beloved beige mackintosh? Well-cut and a firm favourite but even as she slipped it on, she had to admit it had seen better days.

This was becoming ridiculous, assuming an importance it certainly did not warrant. She wanted to look good for him, be honest about that, but it was absurd to overdress and worse still to dress unsuitably. Damn! Trousers again and a heavyweight sweater and forget the dangly earrings. The trouble was she looked about sixteen, not at all a sophisticated lady like Suzanne Roye who was the sort of irritating woman who could make a boiler suit look fetching.

She picked up her hair-brush as the doorbell rang. Never. Surely it wasn't him already? Hastily, she grabbed a bottle of perfume, sprayed it lavishly somewhere in her direction and went downstairs to let him in.

"I'm nowhere near ready," she said by way of greeting. "When you said ten-ish, I didn't think you meant before ten. You'd better come in and wait.' She stood aside as he brushed by, just missing touching her by the merest whisper.

"In here....' She ushered him into the room that doubled as her studio. "Sorry about the smell of paint, it's an occupational hazard." She smiled at him. "I'll be as quick as I can."

When she returned, finally satisfied with her appearance, he was poring over some sketches. "These are good," he said, meaning it. "Have you ever exhibited before?"

She shook her head, beaming at him, childishly pleased at the praise. "The exhibition will be mainly oils. I love oils," she continued, picking up one of her favourite paintings. "Do you like this one? It was early summer and I liked the way the sun was just peeping over the hill as if it was nervous of being too bright." She gently let her fingers drift across the canvas. "I defy anyone to look at this and not be moved. It takes your breath away, nature like that."

"I know the feeling," he said quietly and, catching his glance, she saw he was looking at her, standing quite still but somehow poised. For a moment, she thought he was going to reach out and pull her towards him. It was too soon. Much too soon.

"I'll get my things," she said quickly, heart pounding.

She busied herself collecting together the things she had earlier assembled for the trip. Bag. Brolly. Scarf. Gloves. Wellies. Travelling rug. Flask of coffee. Sandwiches. Chocolate. Sketch pad and pencils if she should get the opportunity. Camera. Tissues. "I think that's everything," she finished brightly, daring to look at him again.

"I sincerely hope so," he said with a grin. "Tell me, Catherine, do you always travel complete with kitchen sink?"

"It may look excessive," she admitted, "but I don't trust weather forecasts and that sky looks pretty full of snow to me. It's touch and go, Adam, whether we should set out at all."

"I think we'll be fine," he said, as they stepped out into the cold. "I'm usually a good judge of weather conditions and I reckon the snow will keep off today." He helped her into the car and smiled down at her. "We'll keep the chocolate back just in case we get stranded. Or have you a flare hidden in that bag of yours?"

He succeeded in making her feel she was overreacting to the weather, but she still eyed the sky anxiously as they set off. She hated snow. Joe had been lost in a blizzard and snow made her panic.

They took a wide, leisurely loop towards the hills. Quickly aware that Adam was a very good driver, Catti allowed herself to relax at last, pointing out little interesting details as they drove past.

"Tell me what you were planning to do with the house," he said, changing gear as they climbed steadily up the narrow, twisting road.

The question startled her. "Why? Do you think it will be therapeutic to talk about something that won't happen now?"

"Perhaps it will. It might help. I'd like to know anyway. I feel curious about it. Surely you weren't planning to live there all alone?"

She debated whether to tell him. It was difficult to think straight with him so very close, the muscles of his thighs straining against the tight cord trousers he seemed to be fond of wearing, a bulky blue sweater covering his upper body.

"I've always enjoyed teaching art," she began at last. Why not? He might be right, it might help. "But when I was teaching in school as I used to, I found I had scarcely any time for my own work, my sketching and painting, and the illustrations were just starting to take off too. So ... I resigned and went freelance after I got married."

"A bit of a gamble surely?"

"In a way." She smiled a little, remembering the dithering before she took the decision. "I miss teaching. I always intended to get back into it somehow, evening classes maybe. When I knew Bay's End was up for sale again, I knew exactly what I wanted to do."

"Go on," he prompted, as she fell silent. Up ahead, a few flakes of snow were drifting towards them, unhurriedly as yet but ominously for all that.

She gave a little sigh. "I realize now, of course, that I never thought it through properly. I was going to live there and offer painting courses. Not exactly a hotel, nothing as grand as that, but...." She shook her head. "What a mad idea! I can't even boil an egg properly. I was going to ask Penny to help out but ... perhaps it's just as well you beat me to it, Adam. I never considered all the practical difficulties. I just had this vision of a few people learning to paint, having quiet chats, sitting down to a relaxed meal."

"It's not too far removed from what I intend to do," he said and she blessed him that he did not laugh at her amateur grandiose ideas. He slowed as the road narrowed further and, all around, there was the haziness of low clouds as the snow bided its time, bundled up, gathering strength. "Except that I've had experience in running a hotel, of course, so that holds no fears."

"You're not going to offer painting courses, surely?" Catti laughed. "Don't tell me you're a painter in your spare time?"

"God, no. Outdoor centre with the house as a base. I've got one or two expert tutors lined up and I'm just getting the financial side of it sorted out. Suzanne...." There was the slightest pause. "My ex-wife by the way, she's putting up some of the cash."

"Is she?" Catti said faintly, still reeling from the oh-so-casual "ex-wife". An ex-wife with money. Just who was using whom? It disconcerted her and yet, she was glad he had told her. The casual way he had mentioned it did not fool her for a moment. She knew he had been rehearsing just how to say it.

"How far is this place we're heading for?" he asked, changing the subject abruptly. "I don't like the look of the weather."

"You're the one who said it would be all right," Catti said sharply. "We're here. Just round the corner. Pull over by the lake."

They were skirting the lake quite suddenly, the road

uncomfortably almost on a level with it. The lake was full, a mere half-inch away, it seemed, from overspilling. Dark and gloomy, moving slightly in the light wind. Catti imagined the contours of the hill continuing beneath its murky waters to produce shallow then suddenly deep water. It was enough to make her shiver as Adam pulled the car over and stopped the engine.

"It looks different," she said into the silence. "Now I think of it, I've only ever seen this place in summer." Her eyes scanned the far shore as she said, turning to look at Adam, eyes shining, "Isn't it fantastic? Would you mind if I did some quick sketching to take back with me?"

"Not at all. Would *you* mind if I left you to it and took a quick walk up the hill?"

"In this weather?" she queried anxiously. "You won't go far, will you?"

"I won't go far," he assured her, climbing out of the car and slipping into a warm anorak. "I can't resist having a peep, that's all." He leaned into the car. "And you'll want some peace and quiet to do your sketch. See you later."

She said nothing, watching until he had disappeared. Visibility was not too good now as the snow thickened and she worked quickly on the sketch before it became impossible to capture the sombre mood of the scene. She was right. It did look different in this light. She had never before thought of the hill that rose abruptly from the lakeside as menacing, forbidding, but it now seemed so, its craggy surface already sifted with snow.

Fatter flakes. Soft and silent. The sketch took shape under her fingers and, thoroughly absorbed, she did not notice time slipping by....

She was just beginning to panic when she heard the crunch of footsteps and he was back, shaking off the snow before climbing in beside her. She tried to smile, not wanting him to see how near to desperation she had become. Alone, she had imagined the very worst. Joe had been lost in a blizzard. For one moment back there, she had allowed herself to consider the possibility that he, too, might be lost. Terror had thudded into her. She had very nearly succumbed to the temptation to set off looking for him, not even knowing where to start. That would have made a lot of sense, two of them lost in the snowstorm.

His cheery grin went some way to dispelling her fears. "Get your sketch finished?" he asked. "Great hill that. Good combination up there as far as I can see. One or two decent overhangs. Moderate to difficult, I'd rate it."

"Would you?" Her self-control was returning, her hands calm on her lap. "I'm very reliably informed that it rates as easy to moderate."

"Depends on your source," he said, looking carefully at her. "I veer to caution and I certainly wouldn't dream of bringing my beginners here."

She stared at him a moment, perplexed, as the awful truth dawned. "Do you climb?" she asked quietly, willing herself to have misunderstood.

It was not to be. "I do," he said proudly. "A bit rusty of late but ..." he shrugged. "I ran a trekking centre for a while in Kathmandu with a friend. I enjoyed it there. I sometimes think I should have stuck it out."

Why hadn't she realized before? There was that look in his eye as he began to talk to her about it, *that* look, a Joe look, that made her look at him dully. No, no.... She couldn't be that unlucky. Could she? Not twice. She could scarcely hear what he was saying as a tightness overtook her, a numbness that had nothing to do with the cold. A strange feeling of not being here, of being somewhere else, snow spinning, catching her breath, suffocating her....

She came to held close against his chest, against the heavy sweater. "Hey...." His voice was so concerned. "Catherine, darling, are you all right? Catherine, please...."

She tried to sit up but she was pinned against him. She tried to say that of course she was all right, that she had never fainted in her life, that she was definitely not a swooning sort of woman, that she....

He was covering her gently with a travelling rug and then there was the sound of coffee being poured from the flask. "Drink this," he ordered, helping her hold the cup. "It's a pity it's nothing stronger. God, you frightened me," he said, his hand warm on hers. "Feeling better?" he enquired softly. "I'm going to take you home. Right now."

The sympathy was suddenly more than she could bear and, to her horror, she felt her eyes fill with tears. That's all she needed! "We're not stuck, are we?" she asked in a small voice. She knew the power of the weather, she knew how quickly a road up here could become impassable, particularly such a high road as this. They seemed to be in the thick of the snow-cloud, scarcely able to see as it dizzied in a bewildering spiral against the windscreen.

"We should never have set out," he said, taking the coffee cup from her as she finished. "My fault ... after all my experience, I can't believe I'd take such a risk." He frowned at her. "I just don't seem to be thinking straight." The look they exchanged was completely honest and, as he reached for her, she almost fell against him, still a bit wobbly. Bulky sweater against bulky sweater. Gently, so very gently, he touched her face, and then his lips followed the same pattern, resting on her mouth, a tender kiss, a loving kiss, a patient kiss. Now was not the moment for anything more. "We'll be fine, my love," he whispered. "I won't let anything happen to you. God, I've only just found you. Do you think I have any intention of letting you go?"

"Adam, I...." She pulled away, turning her face for one last look at the dark lake. "Take me home," she said. "Before it gets any worse."

She worked hard at shaking off the lovely, warm feeling that caught at her. She had to. She had no intention of getting involved any further with Mr Adam Trent. Now was the moment to put the brakes on it. It was quite simple. She had not broken down and confessed her feelings for him. He need never know. He would get over it.

"You're quiet," he said, after a very long time. "Are you sure you're feeling better?"

She glanced sharply at him. "I've been thinking about what you said," she murmured. "About your plans for this activity centre...."

"And?" He seemed puzzled. "Is there a problem?"

"Someone tried to do something similar a few years ago," she said smugly. "I'm afraid he never got planning permission. The villagers put a stop to it. They organized petitions and all sorts of things."

He changed gear with a rapid, decisive movement. His manner changed too, tight now and tense. "Is that supposed to frighten me off?" he said.

"I'm just warning you." Catti wished she could keep a dignified silence. She didn't like herself like this. Why was she doing it? It was as if she deliberately wanted to hurt him, to make it impossible for him to continue to like her, let alone love her.

"If you knew me better, you'd know that I do not respond to warnings," he said quietly. "I'm going through with it and hang the objections. Why didn't you say something before?" He was suddenly driving too fast for the road conditions, wheels spinning as he took a bend too quickly.

"You'll not have it all your own way," she said, gripping the seat. She would not ask him to slow down. She would not. "All hell will break loose when they find out what you're planning."

He laughed but there was little humour in the sound. "I've got a strong case," he said. "I've thought it all through. Nobody's going to be disturbed, the place is far enough away from the village and my visitors won't be indulging in late night parties. And you forget, Catherine, that I have Suzanne Roye on my side. She's not exactly a babe in arms when it comes to publicity. She knows how to win people round."

"And you'd let her do that?" Catti stared at him in disgust. "How can you?" The car lurched and she suddenly screamed at him. "Look, do you have to drive like a maniac?" she shouted, fear overcoming her cool resolve. "Slow down, before we crash."

He slowed down. Miserably, Catti stared out at the

rough, snow-covered landscape, the snow tailing off now as they descended onto lower ground. She wanted to say she was sorry. What an awful way for the day to have ended. And, unless she explained about Joe, he could not hope to understand her change of mood. One minute, she had most certainly responded to his kiss, the next, she was like this....

"Catherine ..." he hesitated, as they entered the beginnings of Chartscross. "What's the matter? Why are we shouting at each other?"

She looked across at his hands on the wheel. Strong hands. Nicely shaped hands. No rings. An ache stabbed at her. *No.* She would not give in to her heart.

"I shall fight you all the way on the hotel business," she told him crisply. "So I wouldn't bother making too many plans."

He stopped the car short of her house and let a sigh escape him. "Why?" he said quietly. "I don't understand you, darling."

"Don't you 'darling' me," she said. "Save that for your ex-wife."

"So that's it," he said, his face clearing. "You think that Suzanne and I are still involved with each other. Wrong. Absolutely wrong. We have no intention of getting back together. She's getting married again in the spring." His smile rocked her heart. "Aren't you going to invite me in for coffee?"

"No." She struggled out of the seat-belt. "If you could just help me get my things together...."

Her iciness finally reached him and she flinched as his eyes clouded with a sort of pain. "Certainly," he said briskly. "In you go and I'll carry all the stuff in. Don't worry, I'm on my way as soon as I've done that."

"Good."

The house was empty. Silent. A sob caught at her as soon as he had gone. She was doing the right thing. No doubt about that. If she reined in her feelings now before it went any further, it would be easier.

She touched her face, remembering the gentle kisses. Then, she braced herself and ignored her heart. She had lost one man to the mountains. She was not going to lose another.

Five

"Post, Miss Benson." Stuffing her duster in her pocket, Grace handed her the letters with a smile. "A phone bill, a circular, and that looks like a wedding invitation to me."

"A wedding invitation?" Catti took the letters from her, fingering the stiff white envelope with the silver horseshoes. Yes, it certainly did look like a wedding invitation, but from whom? She carried it over to the breakfast table and began to slit it open.

Grace, curiosity bursting from every seam of her cotton overall, fussed at the sink. Catti glanced at her, smiling, deciding to put her out of her misery. "Do you remember Stuart Patterson, Grace?" she asked. "A climbing friend of Joe's. He came over to see us once, when we lived at the flat?"

Grace frowned a moment in concentration. Her association with Catti and Joe went back a long way. "I remember him," she said now. "Big man, isn't he? Beard. A real gentleman."

"That's him." Catti thought fondly of Stuart. She had first met him years ago when she and Joe had gone to Scotland for a brief holiday. A holiday that had turned into a get-together with all his old climbing friends. Nostalgic meanderings over late drinks in cosy pubs. Do you remember this? Do you remember that? The lone woman, Catti had begun to feel distinctly left out, but Joe could be incredibly thick-skinned and had not noticed. Despite the slight irritation all these reunions produced, Catti had liked Stuart and that had helped ease the friction between herself and Joe. Stuart, bless him, had done his best to include her in the conversations and she remembered him for that. He was a gentle giant of a man, a botanist by profession with a passionate love of the hills, their flora and their fauna. Sometimes, watching him examine a plant with infinite care, he seemed, despite his size, out of place in the essentially rugged world of climbing.

Since Joe's death, they had kept lightly in touch. A Christmas card. An occasional short, friendly note like the one that accompanied the surprise invitation. Catti read it as she finished breakfast. "He's getting married. Up in Aberdeen."

"That'll be nice for you." Grace beamed. "I love weddings. A new outfit. A hat." She attacked the work surface with feeling. "Mind you, it's not a good time of year for a wedding. Too cold. I like spring weddings myself. Well, well, that is a surprise for you, Miss Benson. Do you know his fiancée then?"

Catti shook her head. Stuart said he wanted her approval. She could see his smile as he wrote that. He apologized for the short notice and he was well aware that most weddings were arranged months in advance, but they had decided on a whim to bring it forward. He was off on a Himalayan climb come the summer and they wanted to fit in a leisurely honeymoon before then. Anna wanted time to get used to being Mrs Patterson.

She propped the card against the sugar bowl and

stared at it. "Anna's Danish," she told Grace. "They're spending their honeymoon there, according to Stuart, where there's not a decent mountain in sight. Anna's idea."

"Sounds a sensible young lady." Grace eyed her thoughtfully. "Will you go?"

"I'm not sure." Her first reaction was to refuse. A polite refusal, of course, nothing to hurt their feelings. After all, it was short notice. There were a hundred and one reasons why she could legitimately turn it down. The distance for one and the sheer difficulty of getting there. A laborious journey by train and a very lone one for a solitary driver. The unpredictable weather was another minus point, particularly up there. And, perhaps the most important reason, she would be alone. A lone female guest. She couldn't bear it if they had invited her with some vague idea of cheering her up or, even worse, of pairing her off with someone, Penny fashion. What would they do with her? People were often paired up at weddings and it might be uncomfortable for her and for others.

Excuses. She gave a sigh as Grace carried on working, glancing at her slyly, waiting for an answer. Would she go? Should she go? Would Stuart and his bride be dreadfully offended if she did not?

"Never turn down a wedding invitation, dear," Grace said quietly. "People don't ask if they don't want you there, not any more. And it'll cheer you up after all that business with *that* house." She now refused to call it by its name. She now called Adam Trent *that* man with some venom in her voice. Catti loved her for that. Grace was fiercely protective.

She hadn't heard a word from him since that day by the lake. He had silently unloaded her belongings from his car, thanked her stiffly and left it at that. She ought to have told him about Joe. That would have gone some way to explaining her odd reaction. After all, through his eyes, what had he done wrong, other than buy a house that she had had her eye on? He hadn't forced himself upon her, his kisses had been painfully gentle. And that was one of the reasons why this was so hard. He was so nice, damn him, worryingly as protective towards her as Grace, as if he somehow cared.

She dreamed about him. She woke up and her first waking thought was of him. In that blissful half-awake state, she had found herself reaching for him in the big bed she had once shared with Joe. She wanted so much for him to hold her close, to cuddle up to him, for him to make love to her, for her to make love to him.

She accepted and deeply resented the fact that she was being absurdly feminine and illogical. She was falling in love. Despite all her misgivings, she was falling in love with Adam. And she must not. She must not fall in love with a man who risked his life as Joe had done. She wanted an ordinary man, who led an ordinary life, nine to five, who could be relied upon to be there when she needed him, feet firmly on the ground. She hoped this Anna knew what she was letting herself in for in making such a commitment. It would need a strong love to survive the separations and worry that Stuart might inflict on her over the years. Just one more climb. The number of times Joe had said that and meant it. Until the next time. Until Stuart offered him a place on the next expedition. A place that could not possibly be turned down.

She would like to meet Anna and talk to her and the only way she could do that was to go to the wedding. Thoughtfully, Catti picked up her breakfast dishes and carried them over to the sink, helping Grace to load them into the dishwasher. "It's a long way to drive," Grace said, a little smile playing round her face. "Aberdeen? Will you stay overnight?"

The hesitation was minimal. "Yes. I'll book a room at the hotel where they're having the reception. That way it will be nice and convenient for me. I'll stay overnight and drive back on the Sunday or ... I might make a long week-end of it and come back Monday."

"Take a week off," Grace said recklessly. "Have a nice break."

"I can't spare a week," Catti laughed. "You'd get me shot, Grace. I do have work to do, you know. I've got to start having some thoughts on my new illustrations. Fantasy. Children's fantasy. Marvellous scope there for me to do something really exciting."

"I'm glad you've decided to go to the wedding," Grace said, quite unnecessarily as her face was full of her enthusiasm for the decision. "You'll enjoy it. And it'll give you an excuse to buy something new. Don't these wedding dos these days stretch into the evening? You'll have to take an evening gown with you."

"I suppose I will," Catti said, carrying the last piece of toast with her into her studio. She was wearing her working clothes, paint-stained jeans and a cotton top and her hair was pulled unflatteringly back into a ponytail. She stopped by the mirror and pulled a face at herself. She would have to make a special effort for the wedding. She was blowed if she was going to have people say that she had let herself go, whatever that meant. She would do something different with her hair. And she would ask Penny to help her choose a new dress. She would splash out on something fantastic.

That decided, she stretched tired limbs and prepared to start work. A thought niggled at her. Should she or should she not go to the meeting this evening that Penny was organizing? Penny was predictably up in arms at Adam's intentions. Penny was a lifelong campaigner at keeping Bordersbay in a perpetual time warp. It was one of the things she and Catti did not quite see eye to eye on. The Anti Activity Centre was about to be formed, with Penny at the helm. Quite a number of the village residents seemed willing to help her and Penny, as self-appointed chairwoman, was taking her responsibilities seriously. Armed with a clipboard, she was already feverishly collecting signatures for a petition to oppose him.

So far, both Don and Catti had managed to avoid signing it. Don, because he quite liked the idea of a climbing activity centre and Catti, because, well ... no, she was not being spineless, she had told Penny, merely realistic. One smallish hotel did not constitute a hotel strip. If Penny would only get off her high horse, she might think about the possible good that might come of it. Penny had accused her point-blank of sitting on the fence. Maybe ... she just did not want to be responsible, even partly, for scuppering his chances, his hopes.

She could not get him out of her mind. Annoying but a fact. When she had fainted by the lake, had she imagined that look in his eyes as she drifted back to consciousness? Had she misheard when she had thought he had called her his beautiful Catherine? No. She had not imagined it. She had not misheard. He had come *that* close to confessing his love. A whisper away. And so had she. But nothing had been said, not a word, and the distance between them now seemed like a chasm. Oh, why didn't he get in touch?

But she didn't want him to, did she? She would only give him the brush-off if he dared to do that. For her to consider a serious relationship, she would have to insist that he give up climbing and how could she ask that? She had once asked that of Joe and he had stared at her a moment and then laughed. She suspected that Adam's reaction would be much the same. He would not love her enough either to do that.

With a little sigh, she set to work sorting through some old sketches. Somewhere, she had a sketch of Stuart which she wanted to give to Anna as a little extra present. There it was! Anna would like it for it captured him beautifully. Although Catti felt more at home with landscapes than portraiture, she had to acknowledge that she had succeeded in the simple pen and ink sketch in conveying on paper what Stuart was like in the flesh.

The three of them, Joe, Stuart and herself had spent a happy day tramping about the countryside, one of those special days that linger in the memory. Taking a welcome rest, sitting on a flattish rock with her jacket bundled up underneath as a cushion, she had pulled out her sketch pad. "No ... just relax," she said, as Stuart caught sight of it and immediately stiffened, assuming the pose he thought she was pursuing. The face was strong, full of humour and kindness. It was all there in the single sketch. She was proud of it and now she would give it to Anna.

She had forgotten about the sketches of Joe. Not quite as good to her critical eyes as the one of Stuart. Something missing from them. An elusive quality that she had not managed to produce. She had married Joe but had she ever really loved him? The thought was a shock in its suddenness, unwelcome. Of course she had!

Adam's face drifted unasked into her mind. Until you were in love, she reflected, you had no measure of what it was like. Very often people made do with something approaching it and they probably didn't even realize it.

With a sniff, she busied herself. Whenever she was overemotional, she needed the solace of painting. Quickly and expertly, she assembled her brushes and varnishes and the squashy tubes of the lovely shiny oils. The canvas in front of her was bare. Temptingly so. She knew what she was going to paint.

A snowscene. With a lake. The view from the car. It was going to be for her eyes alone. Not for sale. Taking a deep breath, she drew on her memory, seeing it in her mind as clearly as a sharply focused photograph.

Unhurriedly now, taking pleasure in the moment, she began to prepare the canvas with a soft wash, fully absorbed so that even Grace's quick in and out in search of a vase went completely unnoticed.

Six

Adam received his invitation, too, in the morning post. He glanced down at the card. The sly old devil! Anna was a great girl, although a little too like Suzanne in appearance for him to feel completely at ease with her. Funny how he was automatically wary of beautiful blondes with pale blue eyes, as if they would all somehow turn into his ex-wife.

Good taste, the pair of them, choosing a Tweed hotel in which to hold the reception. They would do them proud. He knew the one at Aberdeen, one of the newer batch, conveniently if a little uninspiringly positioned at a roundabout on the outskirts of the city.

He did not hesitate. He was definitely going to go and wish the old so and so well on his special day. Good for Stuart. He knew the manager at that particular hotel well, one of the chaps he had himself nurtured for senior management, who insisted that Adam stay in one of the best suite of rooms they could offer. Why not? After the discomforts of the weeks at Whichway Cottage, he deserved a couple of nights in some splendour. And the Braemar Suite was not bad by any standards.

Suzanne's brief call, as he was washing-up, rather took the edge off things. Why the hell had Stuart invited her? He knew they were divorced so why was he taking the chance of embarrassing them? Suzanne was, of course, as much a friend of Stuart's as he was, so, in that sense, Stuart was acting in a singularly civilized manner. Civilized maybe, but damned awkward. They would be together but not together, apart but not apart. It could spoil what had promised to be an enjoyable week-end away from all his present worries.

His thoughts returned to Catharine. His adorable, complicated Catharine. He was most certainly not giving up on her that easily. He would give her a little more time before contacting her again. He was in love with her. It had happened quickly, granted, for him it had happened almost immediately. She had had a truly amazing effect on him. She had, literally, taken his breath away. And she was such a talented lady. He knew nothing about paintings but surely he could not be mistaken in thinking hers were extraordinary. A gentle smile flitted across his face. Never, in all the time they were together had he thought about Suzanne in the same way. And he just knew Catherine felt the same. The mask had slipped momentarily and he had seen the look in her eyes. No woman could look at him like that and not mean it.

He had gone over and over what had happened that day to make her withdraw so suddenly and completely. She had responded initially to his tentative kisses, showing him that physically she did not exactly find him repelling. He had told her about Suzanne, briefly, because he thought it time she knew. Surely that had not been the cause...? It had to be the house. Losing the damned house. Hell, it meant a lot to her. But she need not lose it. If she married him....

Marriage? The thought astonished him. After years of

treading so carefully, he was suddenly absolutely sure that was what he wanted. And he was also sure that was what she wanted too. Why the hell hadn't he told her that he loved her so much? Because he had worried it was too soon, because they hardly knew each other, because he hadn't wanted to frighten her off. Yet he knew with certainty he wanted Catherine to be his wife. Plain and simple.

Briskly, he sprinted upstairs and pulled on a track suit and trainers. Time for a run on the beach to think this over. He had to consider his next move. And the fresh cold air would bring him back to reality if anything would. He had to consider the disadvantages too.

There weren't any. The cold took his breath away, as he set off through the wood to the beach, walking across the hard-packed pebbles to the firm sand. He stood a while, taking deep satisfying breaths, casting his eyes across the miles of grey water towards his mother's home. So far away. An early morning mist was clearing, hanging smokily over the waters, and an early morning sun was hovering worriedly in an ashen sky. There was, as yet, no warmth in it. None at all.

He shivered and began a gentle limbering-up run, concentrating on his own regular breathing, the sand muddy brown and firm. Above him, a gull soared lazily. On one side water lapped. He was surrounded by hills, pushing up determinedly from the coastal plain.

He ran. And ran. Suzanne was wrong about the quality of life. This was what life was all about. An extension of what he felt when he was standing roped on a tricky rock face. Alone. A companion somewhere above, and below. But at that moment, alone. Taking time to take pleasure in nature. How many times had Suzanne stopped to look at a morning sky?

He smiled. A cold winter morning's jog did not usually conjure up such deep philosophical thoughts. Normally he blanked his mind, concentrating purely on putting one leg in front of the other. He supposed he was a shade vulnerable and he knew why. It was because of Catherine. They belonged together and it was high time they both accepted the inevitable.

"Mr Trent.... Good morning!"

He stopped, panting with his effort, looking towards the voice. It was Penny walking a dog, a shaggy leggy mongrel, who was bounding joyfully out to the water's edge in pursuit of a seagull.

She smiled as he approached, clad in trousers, boots and a navy jacket. A bright yellow tea-cosy of a hat added a flamboyant touch. "Hello there," she said cheerfully. "Out jogging?"

"I was." He adjusted to a leisurely amble and Penny picked up a piece of driftwood and threw it for the dog. "Good morning to you, Mrs ... er ... Perfect," he grinned.

She giggled and looked suddenly young. "Call me Penny," she said, retrieving the stick for the dog and throwing it again. "Now ... Adam ... I may call you Adam? ... I'm well aware that I may be accused of fraternizing with the enemy but I think it's time you and I had a chat, don't you? This whole thing's gone on far too long."

They walked over the pebbles to a stretch of low seawall and sat on it. A strong smell of seaweed hung about and they sat a moment in silent contemplation.

"Well?" Adam asked at length. "I seem to have upset you and your friends with my plans. Why, I can't imagine." He looked across at her questioningly. "I intend to be as considerate as possible bearing in mind that it's me who's the stranger and that the rest of you are Bordersbayians to the very core." He noticed her slight smile and ploughed on. "Why don't you step back a moment and reconsider? What harm is it going to do the village? At any one time, my number of guests will be quite small and they'll be coming along for a purpose – to learn about climbing." He indicated the greyness all around them. "It's hardly the stuff of Benidorm, is it?"

"No, it isn't. Thank goodness." Penny bit her lip anxiously. "But it's not just your immediate plans. We've got to think about the future. We let you off this and goodness knows what will happen next. Will you be honest with me?"

"Of course. Fire away," he said, as she hesitated.

"Is it true that you've bought land to the west and that you'll eventually be applying for permission to put a caravan site on it?" She eyed him in a slightly schoolmistressy way. "Now we really are one hundred per cent against that. Tacky caravans littering the cliff...."

Adam laughed. "Hold on.... That is not true. God knows who started that off."

She stared at him. "The vicar's wife actually," she said, joining him in a rueful smile as she saw the funny side. "It isn't true then? Thank goodness." She heaved a sigh. "I hoped it wasn't. Catti said it wasn't. And I didn't want it to be true because I really would have had to fight you tooth and nail on that one." She called the dog and it tore towards them, skidding to a sandy halt, panting, covered in wed mud from the water's edge, eyes glowing, tongue hanging out, radiating happiness.

Adam leaned forward to pat it and its tail thumped energetically. "I wish life was as simple and straightforward for us," he said pointedly.

"So do I." Penny fell silent, rubbing her hands together as the cold penetrated. "It's Catti, isn't it?"

He nodded. "Something's upset her. I don't know what. I'm lying low for a while."

"Honestly, Adam, if you'd made a deliberate attempt to foul things up with her, you couldn't have done it better. She's very upset. Poor girl, she'd set her heart on that damned house this time." Her voice tailed away and it was a moment before she blurted out, "Are you serious about her?"

He raised amused eyes. "You don't beat about the bush, do you? We've not known each other very long."

"So?" She smiled broadly. "Since when has that mattered? I'm sorry, of course it's none of my business. Catti told me as much. She can be very direct sometimes," she added wryly. "It's just that I don't want to see her hurt. She's had a tough time these last few years, losing Joe and everything." She clicked her tongue with exasperation as she looked at him. "You would be a climber, wouldn't you? You lot get everywhere. My husband used to climb a lot," she continued by means of explanation as he looked puzzled. "You're a stubborn lot."

"Ah yes...." He smiled as they began to retrace their steps towards the wood, the dog now loping along at their heels. "We've both been married before ... Suzanne's my ex-wife, did she tell you?... It makes you extra careful. Do you see that?"

"Yes, I see that. Are you still going ahead with the hotel thing?" She shot the question at him abruptly, kicking her way over the rough stones. "If I wanted, I could fight you on it. I've done it before. I can lobby the councillors on the planning committee...."

"So can we," he reminded her gently. "And Suzanne, I regret to say, has influence. I don't like to think I would let her use it but...." He helped her up the slope onto the path. "Was that just a temporary truce then? Is it back to the enemy camps now?"

Penny clipped the dog's lead on. "I must be getting old," she murmured. "I don't think I've got the stomach for a fight. Something Catti said got me thinking what the hell I was up to. And Don – that's my husband – he thinks I'm daft. He's volunteering to help out if you do get started." She smiled a little. "See what I'm up against? But it's not easy to back down when you've got people behind you banging drums."

"It takes courage," Adam said quietly. "I wouldn't have thought you short on that." He glanced at his watch. "Why don't we continue our conversation in more convivial surroundings? Over lunch? I've got business in Chartscross and I intend to have lunch there first. And I want to talk to you about Catherine."

"Catherine? Oh ... you mean Catti...." She looked at him in surprise and confusion. "She's sworn me to secrecy, Adam. She's warned me that if I dare say anything about Joe...." A blush crept on her face. "And I don't know that I should be having lunch with you."

"Why ever not? I'm sure your husband won't mind me stealing you away for an hour or so and I hate dining alone." He grinned at her. "I really would appreciate a few words."

"You're going to try to worm it out of me," she said, pretending to be cross. "Don won't mind at all. He lives in a world of his own. He wouldn't know if I'd been to a garden party at Buckingham Palace. No ... I'm more concerned with what my fellow conspirators will say if they get wind of it. After all I've said about you. It practically amounts to high treason. You're supposed to be the big bad wolf."

"I thought of ringing to book a luncheon table at High Gables. Do you know of it? Someone recommended it," he said vaguely, knowing full well it was the most exclusive restaurant in Chartscross. "I thought you might want to examine their menu?"

"I could teach them a thing or so," she said crisply but he saw she was wavering. She tugged at the dog's lead. "Come on, let's get you back."

Adam watched her departing figure. He liked her. Sturdy. Sensible.

"Pick you up around 11.30," he called after her.

She raised a hand in acknowledgment, her reply lost in the wind.

Seven

They were over the Forth and on their way and Suzanne was still complaining bitterly. Adam changed gear and overtook a slow-moving lorry, before his irritation finally spilled over. "Look ..." he said, "does it matter whose fault it is? Yours? Mine? The fact is we're late. We can't do a damned thing about it. At least we'll be there in time for the dance. Stuart won't mind."

"But I *do*." She adjusted her position on the passenger seat, reeking of a strong scent he disliked, showing a lot of black stockinged leg. "I hate being late. It's incredibly rude of us apart from anything else. We've missed the ceremony. The best part."

He chuckled, casting a quick glance at her. "I didn't know you were into weddings," he said. "You do surprise me."

"Weddings are back in fashion," she said mysteriously. "Didn't you know? With all the trimmings of course. Satin and lace. It's all incredibly romantic." She placed her hand lightly on his and he shook it off impatiently. "Bruce and I ..." she continued, quite unabashed, "we're planning a very romantic wedding. We've written our own vows. It will take place in California overlooking the Pacific. Can you imagine that? Some friends of Bruce's live there. They think I'm terribly famous of course."

"Do they?" He wished she'd flown up. Come to think of it, why hadn't she flown up? She usually flew everywhere. Why all the fuss with trains and car? He had thought it odd when she had asked him to meet her off the train at Edinburgh but he had agreed because it seemed churlish and unhelpful not to.

His mother had warned him to be careful of Suzanne and he was beginning to see why. Bruce this ... Bruce that ... a romantic wedding in California ... and yet, he had the distinct feeling that if he were to stop the car at this very moment and drag her into his arms, he would meet with precious little resistance. He knew Suzanne. He recognized the sexual energy radiating from her. Once ... maybe not too long ago, he might have been tempted. After all, she was a beautiful woman and there had been good times.

"Have you booked in?" he asked, breaking a silence that was becoming oppressive.

"Booked in? Where?" He felt her quick, amused glance. "Should I have? I assumed, sweetie, that you...?"

"I've booked a room for myself," he told her quietly. He knew it. He was a fool not to have realized it earlier.

"Well ... that is nice and considerate. Thank you very much," she said. "What the hell am I supposed to do? Sleep in the street?"

"It might go with your new outdoor image," Adam said calmly, trying not to be ruffled. "But it will be a touch cold up there. You can share with me if you like," he added, knowing that the Braemer Suite consisted of two separate bedrooms linked by a bathroom. In addition to that, there would be a sitting-room-cum-office. "Separate beds," he added grimly. "Separate rooms even. That goes without saying of course."

"Of course. I never imagined otherwise." Her voice was a little strange. "I'm sure Bruce will approve."

"He'll have to. I've no intention, darling, of doing anything dishonourable." He regretted the bitterness of the tone but Suzanne did that to him, damn her.

"Bully for you." Her laugh was short, forced. "By the way, your mother tells me you're off to the Himalayas again in the summer. Whatever for? What else have you got to prove? We all know you're a big boy, sweetie." She paused, letting out a sigh. "You should stop before you go the way so many of them go. How can Stuart contemplate leaving Anna, so soon after they marry? It's so incredibly selfish but then you climbers are all alike in that respect. Incredibly selfish."

He ignored that. He did not want to arrive hot and angry from an argument. "Shall we stop for a coffee?" he asked, as they passed a roadsign advertising a cafe up ahead.

"You are joking? People stare at me, Adam. Is it her? That woman on the telly? Sometimes I feel like screaming. I have to be perfectly turned out the whole time. I can't even go into Sainsburys without feeling that people are eyeing what's in the trolley. Oh, she buys that does she? Bruce thinks it's a hoot. He revels in it. I find it unnerving. I wish ..." her voice was soft, low, "I sometimes wish I was just plain old Suzanne Trent again."

He was startled, allowing himself a quick surprised glance. The mask had slipped. He rather thought she meant it. But it was too late. "Suzanne, I've been meaning to tell you all the way up and now seems as good a time as any ..." he began, irritated to find that he had been a little moved by her revelation.

"You needn't bother. I've guessed. You've met someone else, sweetie."

"Is it that obvious?"

"Absolutely. You've met her but you haven't yet...." She laughed. "I can tell that too. Is she playing with you, sweetie?"

He did not wish to discuss Catherine. Not with Suzanne. He pulled off the road at the cafe and Suzanne cursed, struggling to an upright position, fishing for shoes. "It's all right," he said. "I need petrol. Won't be a moment."

He paid at the kiosk. He had forgotten how pleasant the accent here was. Smiling, clutching a packet of mints, he returned to the car. Suzanne had found the time to apply fresh lipstick and yet more scent. Her skirt was pulled down to a decent length.

"Well...?" she asked when they were once more on their way. "Who is the lucky lady then?" She laughed when he made no immediate reply. "Don't play games with me, sweetie. I know you. You're so intense, that's your trouble. You'll be telling me next you've fallen madly in love with her."

"My relationships are always serious. I don't like playing around."

"Don't be so pompous. Neither do I. A lot of it's just talk with me. You should know that. I didn't sleep with Bruce until he proposed."

"And you're in love with him?"

"I didn't say that. Not that it's any of your business

any more." Her sigh was slight but noticeable. "It seems like a good idea to get married. I daren't tell your mother that we're living together. She's so incredibly old-fashioned. She'd go all huffy and po-faced."

"We're just about there. Plenty of time to get ready for the dance." He slowed for the roundabout. "That's it."

"That? It looks very ordinary. I thought you said it was four star."

"It is. Wait until you get inside before you pass judgement."

He negotiated the roundabout and turned into the car park. "We've made quite good time," Adam remarked as he switched off the engine. "What are you going to wear this evening?"

"Why? Are you interested?" She seemed surprised. "Red taffeta with a black bodice, rather Spanish flamenco. Pity I don't have a rose to put between my teeth...." Her smile was slight as he helped her out. "Shall I save a dance for you, sweetie? The last waltz?"

Her wistful tone was not entirely lost on him. "You know I don't dance," he said lightly, smiling as the immaculately clad porter came to meet them. This weekend was going to be worse than he thought. For whatever reason, Suzanne was out to seduce him. They both knew it. What the hell was she playing at? Did he have to spell it out to her? He watched as she swayed ahead of him up the steps into the enormous brightly-lit reception lounge. Heads turned. People tried unsuccessfully to look discreet.

David came out to meet them personally, grasping Adam's hand, clicking fingers for immediate attention to their luggage, or rather Suzanne's, for Adam had only one overnight bag. Formalities completed, the lift silently took them to their suite. The corridors, too, were silent, thickly carpeted. Fresh flowers and champagne awaited them. As soon as they were alone, Suzanne slipped off her jacket, stepped out of her shoes, trying her damnedest to look tiny and appealing. "I'm going to have a long lazy bath before I do another thing," she told him. Her smile told him a lot. For old time's sake. He could reach out and touch her if he wanted.

"Good idea." He turned away, lightening the moment with a quick grin. "I'm going to have a cup of tea."

She pulled a face. "How very English of you," she said, flouncing off into the bathroom.

Adam waited until he could hear water gushing before removing his jacket, loosening his tie and flopping onto the bed. He was tired after the journey. Above his head was a painting of the sea. A very large picture, predominantly blue and green to tone with the room. He knew nothing about art. He knew the paintings throughout the hotel were part and parcel of the interior design concept. He was not even sure if it was a good painting. All he knew was that he liked it. It was restful. Waves rolling in. White crested waves.

What was it Catherine had said about seascapes? One streak of white, she had told him, and you can transform a painting. It's where you place it that's important. He recalled her voice, an unusual, lowish-pitched, extremely pleasing voice.

He stirred restlessly. If only she'd told him about Joe. If only he hadn't needed to prise the information out of Penny. If he'd known, he would never have done something so cruel as to leave her waiting whilst he went out into the snow. There had never been the slightest danger that day but she was not to know that and, because of what happened to Joe ... it must have brought back the most awful memories. No wonder that she had not been quite able to control her emotions.

He had not met Joe but he recalled the incident. Stuart had been expedition leader and Stuart had been devastated by it. Blame had to be laid at Joe's feet for attempting the impossible, but Stuart had hoisted that responsibility onto his own shoulders.

Adam sighed and clenched his fists. What a bloody mess! He could hear Suzanne splashing gently in the bath. The door was not locked. It was even slightly ajar. He knew what she expected of him but his feelings for her were dead. Cold as ice. He could no more make love to Suzanne than he could stop himself thinking about Catherine.

Catherine's lovely voice ... you've got me out of the bath, she had said indignantly. He imagined her, standing draped in a towel, that gorgeous red hair cascading about her face. And to think he hadn't even kissed her properly. Not yet. But he intended to.

He closed his eyes, tiredness overcoming him. He closed his eyes but Catherine was still there.

Eight

Anna was classically beautiful in heavy white silk, tight bodice, hooped skirt and billowing sleeves. Her long veil was held in place with a head-dress of pink and white flowers. The bridesmaids, looking cold, wore pink off-the-shoulder dresses. Although there was a fair sprinkling of kilts amongst the assembled guests, Stuart was in a well-cut grey suit.

The sun, a pale yellow orb, fluttered in and out of wispy clouds. The photographer was taking ages and the guests were trying hard to keep smiling and not shiver as they waited outside the church.

By chance or design, Catti knew not which, she had been taken under the wing of an aunt of Stuart's, Monica, who was standing suffocatingly close, elegant in a black and white coat and an alarming large felt and feathered scarlet concoction of a hat.

"They ought to wear hatpins, these young girls," she now said smugly, as a girl made an unseemly dash for a large-brimmed straw. "Then there would be no need for such nonsense." She eyed Catti with slight disapproval. "Of course, my dear, you have no such problems," she said faintly.

Catti accepted the implied criticism with a smile. She had chosen not to wear a hat. Instead, she had taken infinite pains with her hair, producing a shining pigtail held in place with an emerald green silk ribbon to match her suit.

"I shan't be attending the dance this evening," Aunt Monica continued, forcing her smile to remain as an icy blast from the mischievous wind hit them broadside on. "I shall attend the reception, of course, but then I must be on my way."

"Do you have far to go?" Catti asked easily, having caught yet another glance from a male guest, who had been blatantly studying her for some time. Instinctively, Catti moistened her lips and smoothed down the suit. He was, she had already noticed, a man built in the Stuart mould with a free and easy smile and loud laugh. Definitely the life and soul of the party type. Not her type at all.

Supposedly listening to Aunt Monica's description of her journey home, she found herself returning his smile, unspeakingly giving him the go-ahead for a possible mild flirtation. Why not? Today, she felt a touch headstrong and an eager escort for the dance tonight was maybe just what she needed to take her mind off ... Adam, damn him.

The photographer, by now slightly harassed, was calling for aunts and uncles to make up a family group and Catti waved Aunt Monica off with relief, turning to find that, in the meantime, the man had managed to insinuate himself to her side.

"How do you do," he said, approving eyes already sizing her up. "Eric Chambers, cousin of Stuart...." He smiled at the question in her eyes. "You'd already guessed that, I suppose, I'm told there is a certain family resemblance. And you're Catti Armstrong, aren't you?"

He gripped her hand so firmly she had to stop herself from wincing. "Tough luck about Joe, wasn't it? Stuart's never quite got over that."

"I call myself Benson now." She smiled up at him. He was, if anything, a fraction too tall for her. She decided not to comment on Joe. Now was not the time to remind anyone of Stuart's involvement in the sad episode. She had never blamed Stuart. Never. "You should have rescued me earlier," she said now, a shade coquettishly. "I've been rather lumbered, I'm afraid."

She indicated the scarlet hat which was bobbing up and down, creating mayhem as the photographer did his patient best to arrange the clutch of relatives around the happy couple.

"I thought you had. You should have told her to push off. Mother appreciates straight talking."

"Mother...?" She felt herself blush, knowing from the amusement in his face that he had deliberately set out to mislead her. "I'm sorry, I didn't know she was your mother."

"How could you?" He shrugged. "No offence taken, I assure you. Oh thank God, they've finally finished. Group photograph and that should be it. Aren't these dos boring? We'll all catch pneumonia. I need a whisky inside me."

He guided her towards the group. Catti smiled at Stuart and Anna but they did not see her. They were taking a moment to look at each other. A private look in the middle of all this. It brought back instant memories of her own wedding. They had had such hopes, she and Joe.

If she was honest with herself, she was not entirely

sure that their marriage would have lasted. Little things. And important things. But, because he had been killed, she was forever linked to him. That was something she could not explain to anyone. Not even Adam.

Adam had looked at her like that. Nothing could take that away. For a moment, sadness dogged her, then it was quickly forgotten as the photographer made a weak joke and called on them all to smile please.

At her side, squeezed together rather unnecessarily, Eric touched her arm proprietorially, urging her not to look so serious. "It's not a funeral," he whispered. "I know it's practically sub-zero but we're supposed to look happy."

Obligingly, she smiled. At the light-hearted words. For the photographer. But most of all, for Stuart and Anna. It was their day and she was not going to spoil it.

She kicked off her uncomfortable shoes as soon as she was back in her room at the hotel. The reception had gone fairly well even if the speeches had gone on a bit too long for comfort. She had found herself sandwiched between Aunt Monica and an equally formidable aunt of Anna's. Unfortunately and surprisingly for a native of Denmark she spoke only poor English and Catti's face ached from all the smiling she had done to compensate for the lack of lively conversation.

Taking off her outer clothes, she lay on the huge bed. This hotel was lovely. Dark blue carpeting throughout, luxurious blue leather seating, big bold pots of flowers, prints on pale blue walls. A job lot, she suspected with a smile, casting a professional eye on the three large pictures on her wall. Definitely bought to tone with the colour scheme rather than for their artistic merit.

The room was quiet. Soundproofed. She was glad, after all, that she had taken the trouble to drive up. Penny was right. It helped to have a fresh perspective. She was not absolutely sure but she felt that Penny was becoming lukewarm about the campaign against Adam. Just one or two things she had said. The trouble was she had set off with all guns blazing and to put a stop to it now would be almost a humiliation.

She was not sure how she was going to while away the next few hours. Funny thing about being in a hotel on your own, there was nothing to do for much of the time. She supposed she could leaf through one of the magazines on the coffee-table or watch television, but she had no inclination to do either. She had about two hours to make herself pretty for this evening. Two long, lazy hours. She pulled her hair free from the plait and shook it loose. She would wear it in a simple loose style tonight as a contrast to the elegance of the plait, and try out some new make-up she had bought.

Setting out the bottles on the dressing-table, she realized she would prefer to be contouring and colouring a canvas. She had a sudden, totally impractical urge to paint using strong vibrant shades. She stared at her reflection, frowning. A little doubt was fluttering around. She had said she would meet Eric downstairs and was now wishing she hadn't. It was a wedding and guests were entitled to make merry but Eric was drinking rather a lot. She hoped she would have no trouble with him. Playing the flirt was all very well if you could handle it and, if things got tough, she only had herself to blame for trying to be something she wasn't.

Idly, she creamed her face, seeing herself as suddenly vulnerable and naked without the make-up. She had been less than honest with Adam. She should have told him the truth. She should have explained that it was far better to leave it at that. Far better.

Flinging a tissue vaguely in the direction of the waste-paper bin, she slipped on a robe and crossed over to the window looking out onto the busy road outside, the sound of its traffic very effectively quietened. A car, a white Morgan she thought, was just approaching the roundabout. A car a bit like his. She turned aside. How stupid! Would she always think of him every time she happened to see a car that looked like that?

When she got back home, she would go to see him and explain everything. Make a clean breast of it. Then she could get on with her life. Without him. She was used to being alone. Although ... if she got through to him how frightened she was of him climbing, he might give it up.

Like hell! Would she give up her painting if he asked her to? Thoughtfully, she went to run a bath, glancing at the dress that looked so innocent on its hanger. She and Penny had gone shopping for it. It was ages since she had worn black and she had forgotten how beautifully it contrasted with the creaminess of her skin. She did not tan easily. She preferred not to, in fact.

The dress was simple, fitting like a silken glove. Tiny bootlace straps. A broad belt that showed off her slender waist. It showed a lot of bare skin. Shoulders. A hint of cleavage. Her back. Softly warm and scented from her leisurely bath, she slipped the dress off its hanger and held it against her. Would it perhaps be a little too much for the amorous Eric?

It needed a careful selection of jewellery and she had chosen a long silver chain and silver earrings. There! She twisted this way and that. Hmmm. The back did swoop away rather. She smoothed it down, shaking off her doubts. It was no use playing the femme fatale for all she was worth and then worrying about showing too much flesh. She could handle Eric. He wasn't her type at all. She could remain perfectly in control of her feelings where Eric was concerned. And he would be a good dancer, she felt it in her bones.

Time to go down. She sprayed a cloud of her favourite floral perfume around her, adding a little extra on her pulse points. She picked up her tiny evening bag and a lightweight silvery fringed stole and slipped on her high-heeled shoes. Then, walking in the careful way her shoes demanded, she started down the corridor towards the lifts.

A door to her right opened and she heard voices from within before she saw anyone. She froze, feeling the blood rush from her head, as she continued to walk towards the half-open door. It was too late to do anything else. She could hardly turn tail and make a run for it. She had to brazen it out. She couldn't possibly be mistaken, could she? But even as she thought that, she knew she was not. She would know his voice anywhere. That voice was capable of making her shiver. She would recognize his whisper through a six-inch wall.

Damn! He stepped out just as she arrived, his polite apology changing to delighted surprise as he looked at her. "Catherine...?"

"Why, good evening," she said, as primly as her spectacular dress would allow. "What a coincidence.

Are you staying here too?"

He hid the surprise well, smiling slightly at the somewhat obvious question. "We've only just arrived," he said quietly. "Awfully late, I'm afraid." He was in no hurry, his eyes lingering on her face. "We're guests at a wedding," he added with a smile.

Through the half-open door, she caught a glimpse of a red dress and long silken blonde hair. Suzanne Roye! She had noted the "we". He was not alone. So much for the denial that they were getting back together. It was just not done to share a hotel room with your ex-wife. Under the circumstances therefore, how fortunate it was that their own relationship had been curtailed. That saved a good deal of complications all round.

He had escorted her as far as the lifts. She pressed the button, looking back at him and smiling as it slid open. "If you'll excuse me, Adam," she said brightly. "I'm with the wedding party too and I'm meeting a friend downstairs."

"I see." Did she imagine it or did his face cloud a little? The cheek of him. Here, presumably, to make it up with his ex-wife but not averse to a little something on the side. "I'll see you later," he said, with the smallest of smiles.

"Perhaps."

The door closed on him and with a faint whirr, the lift began its gentle descent. So, too, did her spirits.

Nine

Eric was waiting for her, lounging against the wall by the entrance to the ballroom. He straightened up as she approached. "Well, well ..." he said, admiration in his eyes as he looked her slowly up and down. "You look fabulous."

"Thank you." She was still reeling from meeting Adam so unexpectedly. Why on earth hadn't it occurred to her that he might be a guest at Stuart's wedding? If she had known, she would never have come.

"Shall we go in or do you fancy a drink first?" Eric looked as if he had already had enough but was eyeing the brightly-lit bar wistfully, his own wish abundantly clear.

"I think we'll go in. Find ourselves a quiet corner," Catti said quickly, her eyes straying to the open door of the ballroom where she could see small intimate tables arranged round a dance floor.

He led her in by the hand. The room was pink and gold with an elaborate ceiling and sparkling chandeliers. The four-piece band was playing a selection of middle-of-the-road numbers and a female vocalist, startling in a cerise fishtail gown was sitting at one side, unsuccessfully stifling a yawn.

They were ever-so-slightly early and the party atmosphere was, as yet, on hold. Catti was relieved to find

Stuart making his way towards them. "Anna's just getting changed," he explained, shaking Eric firmly by the hand and giving Catti a somewhat embarrassed kiss on the cheek. "She wanted to keep her wedding-dress on as long as she could so that everyone had a chance to see it properly. Didn't she look lovely?" They all exchanged a quiet smile. "We'll have a few new faces tonight. Adam Trent's coming ..." he directed the remark towards Eric, "and he's got Suzanne with him. Anna insisted we invite them both along. Suzanne's done well hasn't she? Never off the box these days. Suzanne Roye ..." he said apologetically to Catti, "she was married to Adam."

"Yes I know. We've already met."

"Is he still in the hotel business?" Eric asked, accepting a glass of wine from a passing waiter. "What's happening with those two? They drove up together, I saw them getting out of his car."

Stuart shrugged. "No idea. Off and on I think...." He smiled at Catti, aware that they were excluding her. 'We're talking about a friend of ours," he said. "You said you've met him. He's another climber." He eyed her carefully. "You all right these days, Catti?"

She nodded. "Fine. It gets easier, Stuart. A cliche but it happens to be true." She smiled and touched his arm affectionately. "And you must stop blaming yourself. It wasn't your fault. It was Joe's for being so pigheaded."

"Eric's taken up the sport, too." Stuart cuffed Eric playfully on the shoulder. "Eric has no fear and, believe me, in a climber that can be a disadvantage."

Catti was not sure if he was being serious. Sandwiched between the two large men, she decided she had nothing to fear from Eric. What was the harm in having a pleasant evening with him, a chaste goodnight kiss perhaps, nothing more. Certainly nothing more.

The murmur of voices increased, heads turned, and so did they. "Oh, there's my wife." Stuart laughed. "Over here, Anna."

She came across, dressed in a pale blue dress, her blonde hair piled on top of her head in an attractive topknot.

With Stuart, Eric and a couple of other men engaged in sudden shop talk, Catti and Anna found themselves flung together. Politely, Catti murmured a few words about how much she had enjoyed the wedding and how she hoped they would be very happy together.

"Thank you." Anna smiled at her. "Let's sit down, my feet are, as you charmingly say, killing me." They moved over to a corner table, smiling dutifully at each other, not quite sure how to break the ice. "Stuart's told me a lot about you, Catti," Anna said at last. "Stuart feels very guilty about ..." her cheeks flooded with colour, "... about your husband." There was little trace of an accent. Her skin was translucent, her eyes ice-blue but surprisingly warm. Her smile was very pretty and relaxed. Next to Stuart, she was like a piece of fragile porcelain. "Stuart told me all about it."

Catti nodded, accepting the sympathy silently. "It was a long time ago," she said quietly. She raised suddenly unhappy eyes. "Don't you worry for Stuart?"

"Of course. Climbing is dangerous, is it not?" Anna shrugged pale blue chiffon shoulders. "But then life is dangerous. In any case, I can't change him. I wouldn't want to change him." She looked towards him fondly as a great guffaw bellowed forth from the men. "I'm so sorry about your Joe," she said softly, delicately touching the shiny gold ring on her finger with a sort of wonder. "You've been very brave coming here today."

Catti smiled, not quite trusting herself to speak for a moment. Another guffaw suggested a dirty story and she saw it was Eric who was telling it with great gusto. Anna followed her gaze. "I saw you two together," she said. "Now I would be worried if I had married him. He's too careless, Stuart says. Stuart worries for him. He takes unnecessary risks and Stuart is most unhappy about that. That's why ..." she lowered her voice, a little troubled. "That's why Stuart hasn't approached him about the summer climb. Eric is not that experienced ... at least not in the climbing sense," she added drily. "And Stuart will only have experienced men around him. I'm sorry," she said, her discomfort obvious, "I have no business saying this. Are you and Eric...?"

"No, we are not," Catti said hastily. "We've only just met, Anna. He seems quite nice," she finished lamely, not wanting to explain that she was intending to use Eric as an escort for this evening and then promptly dump him. She was not too proud of that. Around the entrance a group of people suddenly appeared, clustered there uncertainly.

"Excuse me, I must play hostess," Anna said, rising gracefully and going across to them to be met with hugs and kisses. Adam was there. Adam looking wonderful in evening suit and cream shirt. Adam ... accompanied by Suzanne Roye who was claiming all the attention, looking chic in red and black, her hair in a new curly style.

Eric turned to her side. "Sorry about that," he said, putting his arm casually round her shoulders. "Old boys' reunion. It isn't often we all get together."

She smiled, her eyes still surreptitiously on Adam, toes tapping in time to the music, one of her favourite tunes. "Shall we start the dancing off?" Eric asked. "Somebody's got to and nobody seems to be taking the plunge."

"I believe it ought to be Stuart and Anna," Catti protested lightly. "They are guests of honour."

"Stuart's given me permission," Eric said easily. "In fact, he's practically ordered me to. He can't dance and he's too shy to take the floor first. You're a lucky lady, Catti, you've got the best dancer here, most of that lot have got two left feet. It's a miracle they ever get up a mountain."

Catti laughed. He left her with precious little choice and she did love dancing. He was already holding out his hand expectantly and she slipped into his arms, strong arms, as they took the floor. For a few moments, she felt everyone's eyes on them and was grateful that Eric had not been jesting. He was a terrific dancer and she allowed herself to be led around the floor, fitting in with his movements, held quite close, enjoying the experience, the first time she had danced with a man for a long time.

They were soon joined by other couples and the floor became crowded, giving Eric an excuse to hold her closer, whirling her round as the music changed to an up-tempo number. "So you were Joe's wife ..." he said thoughtfully, his large hands beginning to stray across her bare back, playfully tweaking the tiny straps of her dress. "Shame about Joe. A man after my own heart, Joe, a bit of a wild streak in him they did say. Could you control him?"

She wasn't sure what he meant but the question made her feel uncomfortable, her little wriggle of embarrassment unfortunately being misinterpreted by him. She made no reply, suddenly wishing she was a million miles away from the arms of this man. She did not like the sensation of his fingers stroking her back, particularly when she saw Adam dance by, Anna in his arms, and caught an amused glance from him.

"Joe Armstrong...." Eric was not letting the subject drop, the movement of his fingers more insistent, making her want to scream at him to stop. "He had to have one damned last try even though it was suicidal. A saner man would never have attempted it, you know."

"Yes I know." She could feel the animal tension in him, as he drew her even closer. A little wave of panic washed over her. Damn. She ought to have taken the trouble of getting to know this man better before practically throwing herself at him. His hands were faintly and obnoxiously clammy and already he smelled of whisky, making her fight against a sudden feeling of nausea.

"Nice chap though," he went on, oblivious to her antagonism and total lack of response to the caressing fingers. "How long ago is it since he copped it?"

She stared at him stonily. She could not create a scene. Not here. "Over two years," she said, in what she hoped was a dignified voice. She did not want to talk any more about Joe. She was extremely irritated with herself for landing in this hopeless position. What she had to do now was quite simply ditch him but, of course, she needed to do it in a charming, ladylike way. Even if she felt like pouring a glass of wine over his head, she could hardly do that.

"Over two years," he repeated softly, whispering the words into her ear. "And there's been no one else since then?" He waited for the slight shake of her head. "Wow ... that's a long time for a lady as sexy as you, darling, to be without a man."

The music stopped. He released her abruptly and they joined in the polite applause, leaving the floor and returning to the table where he immediately attracted the attention of a waiter to order more drinks. Catti waited patiently casting a glance at his flushed face and excited eyes. This was going to be tricky.

"Well?" he said, raising his eyebrows questioningly, taking a gulp of whisky. The music started up again and people began to drift elegantly back on the floor. Catti took a deep breath, annoyed at the way things were turning out. She debated whether she should pretend she did not understand the remark he had made but decided that would be wasted. They were both adults. There was no mistaking the meaning.

"On the contrary," she said, deliberately brisk, "it's passed quickly. I have a demanding career and that's helped me get over it. As for being without a man ..." she shrugged, "I dare say some women would be delighted to be given that opportunity."

He laughed, downing the rest of his drink. "So what you're trying to make me believe, Catti, is that you're an independent lady and that you can do without it." His hands was very near hers. "I don't believe you," he said.

"I really don't believe you."

The warning signs were there. He was already a little drunk and there was an aggressive bounce about him that was worrying her more and more. Now he had got it into his head that she was somehow desperate for his advances when it was the last thing she wanted. "I'm merely saying I manage on my own," she said, thinking furiously how best to deal with this potentially embarrassing situation. She was damned if she was going to spoil things for Stuart and Anna. She wanted them to remember this evening with some pleasure at how well it had gone. Keep the conversation light and as impersonal as possible. Get him to talk about his work. "What do you do when you're not climbing?" she asked brightly. "I know nothing about you at all." She tried hard to assume an interested expression, as if she gave a damn what the dratted man did.

He took his time about replying, then he moved fast, surprising her, catching hold of her hand. "You don't need to know much about me, do you, darling?" he said, his face twisted into a leer that alarmed her. "I probably won't see you again after tonight. We both know what we want, don't we? We're just ..." he paused, his voice slightly slurred, "just ships that pass in the night."

No one seemed to have noticed her predicament. How could they? Trying to remain composed, Catti looked frantically around. Laughter. Conversation. And the female vocalist had started to sing a softly romantic harmony. Rather beautifully. She had a haunting voice.

Smiling all the while, Catti loosened his grip on her hand. She needed someone to rescue her. Even Aunt Monica would be welcome at this moment, doubly so, for if anyone could sort this man out she probably could. With a start, she realized that Adam was standing watching her, at the edge of a chatty group where Suzanne was holding court.

"Know him well, do you?" Eric seemed to have sobered fractionally as he followed her gaze. "I've caught him looking at you once or twice. How many of us do you know, for God's sake?"

A cold anger raged in her. Instinctively, she made to stand up, resuming her seat as he caught at her arm. They were both smiling. Catti had never felt less like smiling but she persevered stoically. "How dare you?" she hissed. "If you're suggesting...."

"I'm not suggesting anything, darling." His smile widened. "Bit of a tigress, aren't you? He's out of bounds this week-end. He's sharing a room with Suzanne."

"I'm aware of that," she said, perhaps unwisely. Certain things were becoming crystal clear. It was all so obvious now. Adam had been working on a reconciliation with his ex-wife. The intimate dinner for two ... who had he been kidding? Anger rose in her. So ... on the very day when he took her out, when he had kissed her, when he had looked at her with love in his eyes ... he had already sown the seeds of a reconciliation with Suzanne and this week-end, he would presumably take that one step further.

She turned her eyes on him, blazingly, boring into him, so that he met her gaze. She used the opportunity presented to good effect, retaining the icy glare, telling him all he needed to know, before whirling round to face Eric. She would show him. She would show Adam that other men desired her. Smiling, oozing eager femininity, she leaned towards Eric, who, although surprised, wasted no time in drawing her near for a revoltingly slobbery kiss.

"Let's get out of here," he said, when they drew apart. His eyes were bright, glittering, his face flushed. "It's too damned crowded." He was leading her out as he spoke. Catti was painfully aware that Adam had noticed all this. She tossed back her hair in a gesture of defiance, as they stepped out of the ballroom, closing the door behind them.

Oh no. What had she done? How could she have been so stupid?

There was no one about. Think, Catti, think. How could she get out of this?

Ten

"Can we go to your room?" Eric asked. "I'm sharing and Bill's got no finesse. He's likely to come storming in just when...."

His quick and easy grin cut through her. He would take some stopping. She had done everything wrong from the word go. She had teased him, blown hot and cold, excited him, given him the distinct impression that she was his for the taking, that she was the sort of girl who would go for a one-night stand. And now, she was in some trouble. She would have to be very clever. Start off with some diversive tactics maybe.

"Oh I've just remembered ..." she stalled him at the lifts, running a hand through her hair. "We can't go to my room either. I'm sharing too. How silly to forget." She was appalled at what she was saying but the situation was desperate. "With an aunt of Anna's," she said, the comic edge of all this suddenly occurring to her as hysteria beckoned. "She's already gone to bed. She's had a very tiring journey, all the way from Denmark, ferry across the North Sea at this time of year ... can you imagine that...?" Her voice tailed away. She bit her lip and blushed. To her astonishment and perhaps due to intoxication, he believed her.

"Damn." He gave a quick frown and then caught her arm. "No problem," he said, "I know where. Through here...." He put a finger to his lips and peeped with exaggerated caution through a door marked Garden Room. A moment later, they were inside.

The room was softly, romantically lit. A wall of windows showed a gently floodlit patio beyond and then the garden. Plants everywhere. Cane furniture. On the walls pretty ordinary floral prints in lemon and white.

Catti noticed all this, idiotically dwelling on the inadequacies of the paintings, before drawing on all her resources of how to deal with a drunken amorous man. Penny would sort him out. But then Penny would never have been fool enough to land herself in this mess. Reason with him, that's what.

"Nobody will come in here," he was saying. "It's not used at night. In any case ..." he took off his jacket, flinging it onto a chair, followed by his tie. Loosening the buttons of his shirt, he moved towards her, his excitement obvious. "I like an element of risk, don't you? Adds a touch of spice. Just think, we could be the sensation of the evening if we get caught."

Catti sat down before her legs buckled. "I think, Eric, that we should get one thing absolutely clear," she began, sitting as demurely as she could, trying not to give him one ounce of further encouragement. "We seem to be at cross-purposes here. You seem to have got the impression ...," she tried an unlikely laugh, "well, you seem to think that I...."

"Oh come on," he said in exasperation. "Don't start playing hard to get now. You've been asking for it all day. You've been giving me the come-on like nobody's business."

"It was all a dreadful mistake," she murmured miserably, willing him to understand. From next door, she could hear the subdued sounds of the band. The situation was difficult but not impossible. Nothing could happen. She was within earshot of a bunch of people who would come running. Or would they? After all, hadn't they seen her dancing with him, looking adoringly at him, kissing him even ... that purely for Adam's benefit, a cheap trick to make him jealous. How could she? She had been playing with fire and the result – this fiasco – was nobody's fault but her own. She breathed deeply as, finesse finally forsaken, he hoisted her to her feet, his hands heavy on her shoulders and immediately began to fumble with the zip of the dress.

"Catti ... you really turn me on," he mumbled, trying to force a kiss on her, breathing hard, pushing his thighs against hers. He was not a large man for nothing and she cursed her slenderness, her sudden frailty. She could feel his strength, his power. She couldn't believe this was happening to her. This was disgusting. Now was the moment to scream and all she could manage was a sort of anguished croak. Her dress, precarious enough to begin with, was now gliding down her body, revealing her skimpy black underwear. Oh God! She tried to keep a tight hold on the dress and, as she heard the material tear, it flashed through her mind, ridiculously, that that was over a hundred pounds down the drain. As if that mattered.

"Leave me alone, damn you. I don't want you," she hissed, trying to get her fingers, her long nails, to his face to scratch him. She was pinned against the wall now, so securely that she could scarcely move and any movement she did make was only exciting him the more. He tore her bra and, tight-lipped and white-faced with the effort, Catti continued to hold on to the ragged remains of the dress. It was a silent, deadly struggle. If only she could get her knee back sufficiently, she could kick out at him. She felt her nails tear his skin and heard him cry out, his eyes blazing with fury and desire.

"Why ... you little tease," he muttered against her hair. "I know your game, baby. This sort of thing turns you on, does it?"

Suddenly, the weight was gone. Vaguely, she sagged against the wall, as Eric was dragged away. Only then did she realize that Adam was there, a furious Adam, and that now positions were reversed and it was Eric who was held firmly against the wall.

"Didn't you hear what the lady said, you bloody fool. Leave her alone," Adam snarled in a voice she had never heard before. "Hell, Eric, will you never learn to lay off the booze? One of these days...." He let go of him abruptly. "Get out before I kill you."

Catti pulled ineffectually at her ruined dress, as she saw Eric stagger out with a last venomous glance at Adam. Gratefully, weak with relief, she leaned against him as he helped her to her feet. "I'll take you to your room," he said, whipping off his jacket and placing it gently round her shoulders. "Can you walk or shall I carry you?"

She giggled at that, hysteria again raising its head, glad of the support of his arms as he escorted her back to her room. Thankfully, they met no one on the way and she subsided onto a chair once there, while he made her a cup of tea.

"The answer to anything," she murmured, taking the

cup from him with a little smile. The sweetness of the tea made her shudder but she sipped it, not daring to do anything else under his watchful eye.

"How the hell did you get involved with him?" he said after a moment. "He's well known for tricks like that. One of these days he'll find himself up in court. He's a dangerous man." His mood gentled as he looked at her. "Feeling better?" he asked.

Catti nodded. "I'm sorry," she said. "I've been such a fool." She raised tearful eyes, letting herself relax in the chair, the enormity of what might have happened just getting through to her.

"It was meant as a bit of fun," she said. "Stupid, I know. I couldn't handle it. If you hadn't come along when you did, I don't know what would have happened."

"I do. I know precisely what would have happened. You're so innocent, my precious, I can hardly believe sometimes that you've been married." He reached for her cup and placed it on a side table. Then, quite deliberately, with the lowest of sighs, he reached for her. He drew her to her feet and held her close a moment, a long moment, her face nestled against his shoulder, stroking her hair tenderly. And this time, there was no resistance. She simply melted against him, hearing his heartbeat, his ragged breathing matching hers. The threatened tears spilled silkily as he raised her chin and looked down at her with wonder. Then he smiled that wonderful smile of his. "Catherine ... I love you," he said. "You're such a complicated little thing, aren't you? I've talked to Penny. She told me about Joe." He was stroking her face as he spoke, patient with her, whilst a turmoil of feeling within her circled her whole body, making her suddenly long for his kiss. "Why didn't you tell me?" he groaned, cupping her face in his hands, his blue eyes searching hers. "Why? If only I'd known."

"I wanted to but I couldn't," she began, her words fading as, at last, with a little sound of delight, he kissed her. A long salty kiss as the tears mingled. "Adam ..." she drew back, murmuring his name shyly, her smile tremulous. "I think I love you, too."

"Only think?" he queried happily, his hand roaming over her back now in tantalizing circular movements. Suddenly, gruffly, he pushed her away. "Sort your dress out," he said. "You've had a shock, having to deal with that clown downstairs. You need to rest a while. I'm not going to take advantage."

Dazedly, shimmering still from his touch, she adjusted her underwear and dress to some semblance of decency while he turned his back, feeling lost as she was deprived so abruptly of his warm nearness. He wasn't taking advantage of her. She wanted him. Desperately. She understood his control. Admired it. Of course. But wished none the less that....

He was slumped opposite in a chair, returning his gaze to her as she returned to her chair, having slipped a silken robe over her tattered clothes. "Tell me about the climbing," she said at last, after a long yet buzzing silence. "I want to know all about it. Did you know Joe?"

"No. Our paths never crossed. As I told you, I spent quite some time away from England when I was younger." He sighed, his elegance crumpled slightly now, his bow tie pulled loose, the top two or three buttons of the cream silk shirt undone. "I needn't tell you how important it is to me. I suppose you could compare it to a drug. Once you've experienced that feeling, up there ... it gnaws at you." He frowned, trying his best to make her understand something she knew she was incapable of understanding. "I've not done as much climbing these last few years as I would have like but, now that I'm going into business on my own, I ought to be able to organize my life so that I can make time for things I want to do. Stuart's invited me to go on this summer climb of his. I think I finally decided tonight after meeting Stuart again that I will go. I need to get back in the thick of things."

"I see," Catti said dully, a coldness beginning to clamp itself around her, chill replacing the heat of longing in her veins. "And I don't suppose anything will make you change your mind, will it?"

There was a short unhappy pause.

"My precious love," he said quietly and her heart leapt at the sincerity of the phrase, "are you asking me to change my mind?"

"I wanted Joe to and he wouldn't either," she said helplessly, exasperation and despair edging her voice. "I begged him not to go that last time. I just knew he shouldn't go. But he went," she finished bitterly. "He went."

"It's not as if it's just a hobby," he went on and she knew he was trying to humour her. "You're asking me to give up something that means an awful lot to me. And, if you're worried about danger, don't. There's danger all around. We have to live with it."

"Joe died," she said flatly. "Up there. Somewhere. In a blizzard. What must it have been like?" She stopped, seeing again her nightmare of powdery snow, hearing his laboured breathing as he struggled, tried to find his way back to camp. She managed a tight smile but it faltered as her lip trembled. "Don't you die, too," she whispered. "Adam, I couldn't bear that."

The distance between them was alive, aglow, and Catti knew all she had to do was to hold out her hand to him. She stopped speaking, all the pleading remaining in her eyes. She couldn't do any more.

"Let me think about this. Please, Catherine. I want to please you more than anything in the world but...."

"Don't bother to say it," she said crisply, tugging free of her emotions. Damn the man! He was every bit as stubborn as Joe. "You'd do anything for me *except* give up climbing," she finished, seeing from his face that she had spoken the truth. "Wouldn't you? Admit it," she challenged, eyes flashing, feeling her heart pound as he stood up and came across to her.

"Come here," he said, opening his arms. Smiling.

"The hell I will," she yelled. "You've just said you love me, dammit, then prove it. If you won't do that little thing for me, then it's over. Finished." She stopped, furious that her voice broke at the words. "You might as well get out now," she added, standing up, shoeless, inches short, definitely not in a good negotiating position.

"Have you heard me?" he said gently, not reaching for her, his eyes clouded now but with no anger in them. "I don't believe that you want to end it, my love. We haven't even started yet and I love you. We will be fantastic together." His smile was a little shaky. "You know it. I know it."

She stared blankly at him, her thoughts in a whirl, a torment. But if he loved her, surely ... "I wish I could believe you," she said.

"You've got to."

She saw that she had. Unable to stop herself, trying to ease the pain, she moved willingly into the shelter of his arms, closing her eyes, feeling the warmth of his love, the strength of his desire. "I don't want you to think I'm taking advantage of the situation," he murmured against her hair, moving a few long strands aside so that he could plant a little kiss on her ear. "I know you're still in shock...."

"Will you stop that?" she murmured, nudging herself closer, slipping her hands underneath his jacket, feeling his broad back through the thin shirt. "You are not taking advantage. I love you and I want you."

He pulled slightly away, his eyes asking a question to which she gave a little nod. Now? Of course now. She had waited long enough for this.

"Won't people be wondering where we are?"

She didn't know why she said the words, but saying them reminded her where they were and that downstairs there was still a party going on. And that Suzanne was at that party. It was enough to dispel the dreamy, romantic mood, the longing for him, and she pulled away with a little cry.

"Where does Suzanne fit into all this?" she asked. "Just what's going on, Adam?"

He made to reach for her again but she held up her hands and he stopped dead, his face twisted into an attempt at a smile. "Suzanne is my ex-wife. You know that. What the hell has that swine Eric been telling you?

That we're still together? Oh, come on Catherine, do you think for one moment I'd be doing this...." He sighed and ran a hand through his hair.

"It has been known," she said, fighting hard against another wave of warm fluttery feelings, "it's called two-timing, I believe."

He laughed. "We are divorced," he said. "It's finished. She's here this week-end because Stuart invited her. She's sharing a suite with me because, as usual, it never occurred to her to make any arrangements herself. Separate bedrooms." He smiled thinly. "Does that set your mind at rest, darling? She's marrying again in the summer."

"Is she?" She hardly dared hope. "Then you're not going back to her?"

"I certainly am not. She's changed too much. Oh ... there were good times, I won't pretend otherwise. Not any more. And I love you, Catherine. Not Suzanne."

"Do you? Do you honestly?" It was only a few steps into his arms and then she was being held again.

"That satisfy you? Or do I have to convince you some more? I have a very good line in convincing," he added with a quick, heart-stopping grin.

It was time to be honest. It was time for all the stupid doubts to be banished. It was time. Her body was in a high state of response, her nerve-endings sending out signals too sensitive, too powerful, to ignore. It was time.

She entwined her arms round his neck and gazed up at him. "I love you," she said, before surrendering herself completely to him.

Eleven

Catti awoke. Alone. Remembering. She lay quietly a moment, warm and relaxed, a contented smile on her face. She had never known it could be like that. It had never been like that before. She absolutely adored him. And the wonderful thing about it all was that he adored her too. He wanted to marry her. And, somewhere along the line, during the long, long night, hadn't she said yes?

She stretched and smiled. She could not wait to get home to tell Penny. Penny would be delighted. Of course, there were still some fiddly little details to be resolved. Penny's campaign to be squashed, although she had the feeling that might not be too difficult with Penny's righteous indignation wavering. Nothing would go wrong. It was impossible for her to feel like this and for anything to go wrong. Last night, Adam had finally promised that he loved her so much that he would do anything in the world for her. He had promised.

And, surely, by implication, that included *not* going on this climb in summer. They might well be on their honeymoon, too, by then. She would have him to herself, to have and to hold and to keep safe. She did not care that the other wives might accuse her of being selfish. Too bad! Selfish maybe but she would still have him. She had made one sacrifice already and one was enough.

Her early morning call startled her. She sat up in bed, pulling the duvet up to cover her nakedness and answered it with a thank you. A note was propped by the phone. Smiling, she read it. From Adam. He had quite dreadful handwriting but she could not fail to decipher the "thank you for making me so happy, sweetheart. I love you" at the end of it.

Holding it against her heart a moment, she folded it carefully and placed it beside her bag. Something to treasure. His first love letter.

Quickly, she showered and dressed in a comfortable loose sweater and trousers. She would not see Adam today as he had to drive down to London on business, so, after a leisurely breakfast, she would be on her way too. She would enjoy the journey home. She would think about all the plans. Mrs Catti Trent. Yes, she rather liked it. Mrs Catherine Trent rather. She liked that too.

The dining-room was half empty, discreet classical music softly circling the room. An enormous buffet held centre stage. Fruit juices. Grapefruit. Prunes. Cereals. Eggs. Bacon. Sausages. Tomatoes. Cold ham. Cheese. Yoghourts. Catti ignored it, settling for toast and a pot of coffee, taking a table by the window, looking out onto another cold, clear day. The sky looked quite different this morning. Everything looked different.

"May I join you?"

Looking up in surprise, she saw Suzanne Roye standing above her, smiling, immaculately made-up, wearing a sunshine yellow suite, her hair so elaborately arranged that Catti wondered if she had a personal hairdresser tagging along somewhere. Either that, or she must have risen at the crack of dawn.

"Of course you may." She felt her heart pound with guilt. Did she know? Could she possibly guess? Surely not and what did it matter if she did? It was very private, between herself and Adam, no one else. Nevertheless, she felt awkward and kept her face averted.

"Adam was off very early. Some God-forsaken hour. I'm flying back." Suzanne gave a huge yawn. "Personally, even nine o'clock is too early. I'm a night bird. I'm wide awake and unbearably cheerful at about one o'clock in the morning. It used to drive Adam mad." She broke off to order tea and toast before resuming the carefully casual chat. "I would sit up in bed beside him whilst he tried to sleep." She eyed Catti shrewdly, forcing Catti to meet her gaze. "So you are this Catherine he's mentioned? The new woman in his life...."

Catti gave a non-committal smile. She was trying not to react like one of Suzanne's interviewees, nervous and tongue-tied, prepared to be humiliated at any moment.

"Adam and I were married for years," Suzanne chatted on, the voice familiar, the blue eyes sharp. "Just after he came back to England. I was a journalist on a provincial paper. I did a very bitchy column." She smiled broadly. "I may branch out into writing novels when I get bored with television." She paused as her breakfast arrived and the waitress, eyeing her with undisguised admiration, fussed and rearranged the lay-out of the table. "Thank you, that's fine," Suzanne murmured eventually, keeping hold of her smile, before turning back to Catti. "I think Adam resented my success, even though you could say he's been successful himself in his own field. So you are Catherine ... Stuart calls you Catti ... which do you prefer?"

"Adam calls me Catherine."

"He doesn't like abbreviated names. He always calls me Suzanne." She laughed and a few heads turned from nearby tables. "I'm always curious about his women," she said quietly. "I find it so amusing."

Catti could feel her earlier euphoria slipping away. She grasped at it in vain. What did Suzanne mean? *His women?* "Has he had so many?" she asked brightly.

"I've lost count. He uses them and discards them as easily as confetti. Once he's had his evil way," she said with a broad smile. "His affairs, Catti, are so utterly predictable. They always follow the same pattern. Let's face it, he's never really happy unless he's stuck up a mountain somewhere. He wasn't meant to share his life with anyone." She sighed, spreading marmalade on her toast. A huge solitaire diamond on her finger caught a flash of early morning light and sparkled. "We had a long discussion in the early hours of this morning. When he came back from being with you...." She bit into her toast. "He's quite a man, isn't he?"

"I don't want to discuss it." Catti started to get up, struggling a little as she found her handbag had managed to insinuate itself around the chair leg.

"Sit down. I haven't finished," Suzanne said, pouring her tea from the silver pot. "Adam and I are going to have another go at it. Whatever's happened between you two, whatever he's said, whatever he's promised, you would do well to forget it, Catti. That's just Adam. He comes running back to me in the end."

Catti tugged the bag fiercely from the floor. After last night....

"I'm so sorry to disillusion you," Suzanne went on

calmly. "You looked so dreamy sitting here. You looked like I hope Anna looks this morning. I know, you needn't tell me, he has that effect. He makes you feel like you're infinitely precious, the only woman on earth." She wiped fingers on her napkin. "We're meeting in London to discuss the arrangements for a reconciliation." She stood up, pushing back her chair with finality. "Once again, I'm sorry to spoil things for you but you had to know and it might as well be sooner as later."

"Is everything all right, madam?" the waitress enquired, removing Suzanne's discarded dishes.

"Everything's fine. Thank you."

"She looks different in real life, doesn't she? Prettier, I think. Hasn't she got lovely skin?"

Catti nodded her agreement. She had to get out fast before she started crying. She was determined not to cry about him. She would not give him the satisfaction of being upset.

It would be a long, long drive.

Adam, too, had a long drive and he rubbed his neck to ease an ache, as he climbed out of the car at his destination. He knew this, whatever it was, would be a complete waste of time, but, with Suzanne chipping in some of the money on the venture, he had to pay her some heed. He had been giving that matter some careful thought. A bad idea. He would have been far safer with a neutral backer and this might be a good opportunity to tell her as much. He wanted to get it over with as soon as possible so that he could get back to Bordersbay and to Catherine. He was longing to be with her again. Last night had been the most wonderful night of his life. He had never known a woman could be so warm and loving and tender.

He locked the car, putting off the moment. It was very quiet. He might be forgiven for thinking he was in the country instead of a short drive from the city.

Bracing his shoulders, he walked smartly up to the front of the warm redbrick house and knocked on the door. It wouldn't surprise him at all if a butler answered it. Suzanne liked the grand life. Odd thing, all this toing and froing. The travel arrangements this past week-end had foxed him. Why had it been necessary for Suzanne to make such convoluted arrangements for the journey when she had intended to fly back? Surely it would have been simpler and quicker for her to fly up, too?

"Oh, do come in, Adam old son." Bruce opened the door wide, shutting it quickly after them to keep in the warmth. "Cold out, eh? What was it like in Siberia?"

"A few degrees colder than here," Adam said pleasantly, stepping into the square-tiled hall. Plants in beautiful containers. An elaborate carved banister. Red carpeted stairs leading to the upper floor. "Suzanne back yet?"

"Hours ago but she's swanned off somewhere. Shopping, I think. You know Suzanne." He raised very pale eyebrows. "We both know her. She never thinks of telephoning. Come on through. Drink?"

"A mineral water, thanks, I'm driving." Adam sat gingerly on a buttercup yellow and white striped silk sofa. It was one of three in the room arranged in front of a marble fireplace, a cosy conversation corner in what was an enormous drawing-room. Suzanne's taste was everywhere, in the pleated, ruffled lemon curtains, in the Chinese rugs that lay on the polished light oak floor, in the carefully chosen antiques. Adam accepted the glass of water, ice and lemon with a smile and settled himself a little more comfortably. "What's so urgent, Bruce? According to Suzanne, it was a matter of life and death at the very least. That's why I've driven down in one day. Some journey that! I'm whacked."

"Urgent? Did she say that?" Bruce lit a small cigar. "Sorry, I can't remember if you smoke?"

"No thanks." Adam sipped his drink with resignation. "You're going to tell me now that it's not urgent."

"Everything's urgent in our lives, old son. The stress is unbelievable. Everybody's at it like there's going to be no tomorrow. Schedules. Meetings. Meetings about schedules. Change of schedules. If you ask me, if we didn't try to do the impossible and work so far in advance, there'd be less reasons for all the panic." He puffed on his cigar enjoyably. "If it was up to me, I'd live smack in the heart of the city, nearer the job. Commuting's a trial. Nose to tail. Fumes. Wish to hell I had your courage. Wish I could say to hell with it and swan off to some place up there. Back of beyond stuff."

Adam smiled at the wistful note in his voice. Bruce would last about two minutes in Bordersbay. "Oh the joys of the rat race," he said. "Suzanne loves city life. She likes to be in the thick of things."

"Ah yes ... Suzanne." He eyed Adam thoughtfully. "The trouble with Suzanne, Adam old son, is that she's still married to you. Oh I know you're divorced. Officially. But she won't accept it. She's been getting more and more edgy lately, short-tempered ... more so than usual, that is. Before she went up to Scotland, it all came to a head." His sigh was imperceptible. "She's not going through with our marriage. The wedding is off."

"But she was telling me all about it. California, isn't it?"

"Was." Bruce smiled ruefully. "So she didn't manage to get round you this week-end? I don't know what she was planning but I could hazard a guess." He flicked the cigar towards an ashtray, his tone troubled. "We're keeping this place. It's worth a bit and we'd be fools to sell just now when the market's down. It'll fetch a quarter of a million someday." His attempt at light-heartedness did not fool Adam. Suzanne was damned good at this, cutting people down to size, letting them down with an almighty thump. "We'll still be working together so we have to stay on amicable terms, even if our relationship's down the Swanee."

"Is this why she asked me to come down?" Adam asked incredulously. "All that way just to tell me something she could have told me there. I hope you're not hinting I should take her back, Bruce. I don't want her back."

"Thought not." He seemed to derive some small satisfaction from that. "No ... it's business. I want to talk to you about being in one of the new programmes. This new slot of Suzanne's. People are so used to seeing her on screen looking like she just stepped out of *Vogue* magazine and we thought it would be a bit of a shock to see her in a completely different mode."

"I can't see Suzanne enjoying that," Adam said drily, "she might get her hair messed up."

"Ah ... you underestimate her. It's all about ratings, old son. She'd do anything to get the top slot. Well ... Suzanne was talking to Stuart up there and your mother, too, I think she said, and they put this idea in her mind. What would people think if Suzanne Roye went up the Himalayas? Bit of a turn up for the book, eh? They'd watch the damned programme just to see if she gets her hair messed up. Don't you see? So we're planning to come with you to do some on the spot interviews."

Adam grinned. "You must be joking. I am not talking to my ex-wife roped to a rock face. You can forget it. It'd be suicidal. It may not be Everest but it's no Sunday afternoon stroll either."

"You misunderstand," Bruce said with exaggerated patience. "Can you seriously imagine her up a mountain? She can't stand heights. No ... the idea is a series of interviews, probing the soul type of interviews, on the run out. Step by step so that the viewer will really catch the excitement of the planning stage. As you pack. On the plane. On the approach. Under the stars."

Adam's laughter rang out. "Have any of you ever been on a climb? It's not romantic."

Bruce did not seem to hear, his eyes glowing now as he outlined his plans. "Don't you see, old son, how the viewer's going to feel? There he is bless his heart, sitting in the comfort of his armchair, cigar, glass of wine, watching you lot risk all. He'll be with you, rooting for you." He paused, tapping his cigar onto the ashtray. "Pity you'll not be in the lead team. Bit of an anti-climax that. How do we get through to the viewer that you'll only be there as a sort of glorified porter?"

"Hardly." Adam hid his irritation. He decided not to pursue the matter, switching the attack to Suzanne. "Why didn't she ask me herself? She had plenty of opportunity to ask me a straightforward business proposition."

"She was trying to persuade you." He raised eyebrows, his smile amused. "I'm surprised she didn't. What's wrong? Don't you fancy her any more?" He checked his watch as a fragile clock on the mantelpiece chimed the hour. "Is that the time? Where is she?"

Silently, Adam fumed. He was damned if he was going to start an argument here and now. It was all crystal clear now. Suzanne had set out to worm her way back into his life, perhaps for personal satisfaction but more likely for sound business reasons.

"You weren't the first choice, old son," Bruce said calmly. "Third in fact. Stuart Patterson first, of course, the expedition leader, the man of the match as it were. Then one of the lead climbers. Articulate bloke. Welsh. Then you."

"I take it they turned you down too?" Adam asked with a wry smile. "You're not having much luck, are you?"

"What is it with you people?" Bruce asked, suddenly angry. "Thought you were scratching around for funds. Sponsorship. I'm offering you money on a plate and you suddenly go all coy and choosy." He cast a sly glance at Adam. "Or is the truth, in your case, that you really can't trust yourself to work with the delectable Suzanne?"

"Do you really want the truth? Because I'm going to give it to you now ... old son." Adam's voice was tightly controlled, dangerously quiet. "I don't love Suzanne. I don't even like her. I don't like the way she exploits people. When she started, believe me, I was so proud. I wanted to tell everyone .. hey, that's my wife. That was before she started to change. Was it your idea to make her as she is? Abrasive. Downright nasty. Uncaring. Rude. It rubbed off. She damned well became that way off-screen as well as on. I couldn't live with her any more. She killed our love stone-dead."

"Adam ... really." Bruce laughed harshly. "People love her. She was voted Woman of the Year. She's gritty, she gets to the heart of the matter. Okay, she might occasionally make interviewees squirm, but that's show business. There's nothing sordid about it. We all have a nice cup of tea afterwards in the hospitality lounge and all is forgiven."

"And that makes it fine, does it?" Adam could not contain the sour note in his voice. "Digging the dirt in the best traditions of the worst tabloid. I wouldn't watch that programme from choice if it was the last one on earth."

"Really sweetie ... you do surprise me. Why didn't you tell me before that you didn't care for the show?"

He had not noticed Suzanne enter the room. She threw keys carelessly onto an antique desk. "Bumpy flight," she said. "And then I went shopping and out to tea. Sorry I'm late." She glanced once more at Adam. "Shall I make the guest-room up for you?"

"No. I'm going straight back." Adam rose to his feet. "I've got a long journey ahead of me."

"Adam's turned us down flat," Bruce said grimly. "I think we'd better forget this idea. Uncooperative lot. We'll go for the potholers instead, although it won't make such good television."

"Be a sweetie, Bruce, and fix us some coffee, would you?" Suzanne flopped onto the sofa, patting the place Adam had vacated. "Oh do sit down and stop being such a baby. I want to talk to you."

"And I want to talk to you." With a frown, Adam sat beside her, his face tight but controlled. "I've got something to tell you. I'd rather tell you to your face than in a letter."

"My, my, that sounds ominous. I suppose Bruce has told you that the wedding's off. Did he say why?"

"I don't think he knows why." Adam looked at her. Oh, how he wished Catherine was here with him instead. He wanted her with him. He wanted to hold her in his arms. And love her again. He should never have left her up there in Aberdeen to make her own way back home. He had to sever the links with Suzanne completely. It was the only way.

"Oh Adam ..." she said after a moment. "Surely you know why?"

"It's too late," he said softly. "I'm sorry."

He thought she was going to burst into tears. He had to get out fast. He could feel her twisting a silken thread, drawing him back into the past towards a veil of memories, some of them pleasant. It was time to be brutally frank. It would hurt her but it had to be said. "I'm sorry," he repeated, seeing the words hit home at last. "I've met someone else and I love her ... I love her very much. She's gentle. And I think she's beautiful. And she loves me." That was it. That was all. "You and I are finished. There's no going back." He looked solidly at her. Straight.

She looked as if she had been hit on the jaw but only for a moment. She began at once to rally round, doing what she did best, taking refuge in anger and sarcasm. "Damn you," she said. "Damn you and your incredibly cute little red-head. Oh, by the way, my wedding's on again. Might as well. I'll be very comfortable with Bruce. No scratching around trying to make a success of a hopeless little business." She glared defiantly at him. "I see now how utterly hopeless you are. Steeped in little home-town values. With a home-town mind. Content to stay in that dump of a place. Well, that sort of thing's not for me. As of now, I'm withdrawing all my financial support. You'll have to do it on your own, Adam, without me holding your hand."

"It was never a question of your holding my hand," he said quietly, refusing to yell at her. "I thought it was purely business but I understand now that I was wrong. I'll have no difficulty getting the money from elsewhere and perhaps it is best if we now go our separate ways. Mother was right," he mused as an afterthought. "She had her doubts about the wisdom of it."

"To hell with your mother," she screamed, her face contorted with her anger. "I don't give a damn about her opinion. Oh ... by the way, I nearly forgot ..." she put a supposedly sweet smile on her lips, "you may find your cute little red-head is just a teeny bit off you when you see her again."

"What have you been saying to her?" Adam asked, curiously numbed by Suzanne's outburst, feeling only a kind of wearisome pity towards her. He wanted to be away from here, away from Suzanne.

"She and I had a girlish chat over breakfast. She was sitting there, sweetie, looking as if butter wouldn't melt in her mouth, like a little blushing bride. That's where you were until the small hours, isn't it? With her." She raised triumphant eyes. "The point is, she swallowed everything I told her. Sat there looking bewildered. Believed it all. She believed it even though I hardly believed it myself."

"I say, bad moment?" Bruce stood enquiringly at the door, comically domestic with a tray of cups and pot of coffee.

"Not at all, darling." Suzanne waved him in airily. "Adam can't be persuaded to stay," she said. "He's anxious to get back up north for some reason."

Her laugh followed them as Bruce escorted him somewhat shamefacedly to the door. "She takes things hard," he said, by way of apology. "Doesn't mean half of what she says. Don't worry. I can handle her. I love her, you see," he added with a grimace. "Damned true, old son. And sooner or later, she'll end up loving me too."

They shook hands. "Good luck!" Adam said, meaning it.

It was stupid and foolhardy to drive all the way back. He was tired. He would book in somewhere overnight and start off in the morning, refreshed. The motel room was adequate. He tossed his bag on the bed and immediately reached for the telephone.

"Catti Benson."

Her voice sent a sensation of joy streaming through him. "Catherine," he said, smiling into the phone. "I'm on my way home."

He knew she was there. He could hear her sharp intake of breath.

He was left staring, his smile wiped away, as she replaced the receiver with a very final click.

Twelve

"She hung up on me." Adam shook his head in disbelief. "At first, I thought it was a mistake but when I tried again, she did precisely the same thing." He looked to Penny for support, for some glimmer of hope. "Sorry to drag you out on a day like this," he apologized, suddenly realizing that Penny was sitting opposite him, still steaming from the drenching she had received outside. "But I thought if anyone could talk some sense into her, you could."

"I hope you're aware that you've ruined my hair-do," Penny wailed, picking at a wet strand. "Mind you, I was glad of the excuse to get out. It's utter chaos in my house just at the moment ..." she paused and smiled. "I hope I can help. I've never seen her so miserable, Adam. Since she got back from the wedding, she's been like a wet rag. She's driving me nuts if you must know. She's shut herself away in that damned studio, slapping paint on canvas for all she's worth."

"Has she said anything?"

"About you?" She sighed. "I don't want to stick my nose into things but I seem to be involved anyway. I'm the go-between, aren't I, whether I like it or not. Would you like to tell me your version of events? Not the details of course...." She flushed and looked intently at the menu.

They were lunching again. A new, self-conscious restaurant in the new, self-conscious shopping arcade in Chartscross. Air-conditioned. Full of plants and slippery, tiled floors. Like another planet. Anything could be happening in the world outside and no one would be any the wiser.

"My ex-wife's managed to put her well and truly off me. I asked her to marry me and she said yes. And now...." He shrugged. "What do I have to say to her?"

"Catti is a fool," Penny said firmly. "I ask you, who but Catti would believe the words of an ex-wife like Suzanne, who's obviously still madly in love with you and out to get you back?" She cast a sly glance his way. "Thought as much. Now ... take me for instance ...if this bitchy ex of yours had tried that on with me, I'd have told her what for. But then I'm no lady like Catti," she added with a quick smile. "Catti was born into the wrong age. She goes more with crinolines and fans, don't you think?" She smiled towards him. "Don't look so stricken. We'll sort it out."

"I don't know that we can. Quite frankly, even if you do persuade her that Suzanne was just out to make trouble, there's still too big a rift. She wants me to give up climbing...." He paused, twisting the stem of his glass. "In the heat of the moment..." he looked up and they exchanged a gentle smile, "I do believe I said I would. It was only later in the cold light of day...."

"Oh. I see." Penny stared thoughtfully at him. "She would, of course. It's Joe. She's scared rigid that she'll lose you. She's frightened of getting involved again and having to go through all that pain. I suppose it's understandable ... she's a very sensitive girl, Adam ... but she's wrong. You mustn't even consider it."

Adam looked at her. At the bright, intelligent face. At the concern in the grey eyes. He liked Penny. He saw why she and Catherine were such friends. "I envy Don," he said now, quietly.

"Thank you. Do you know that's one of the nicest things anyone's ever said to me." Her smile was wistful. "I'll talk to her," she said. "But she can be very awkward when she sets her mind to it. She's decided she doesn't want you in Bordersbay. She's taken over the campaign where I left off. She thinks that Suzanne will be moving here to be with you. And I don't think she can bear that."

"She can forget the campaign," Adam said stonily. "I'm seriously thinking of pulling out of it. I'm beginning to wonder if somebody's trying to tell me something. I don't think Bay's End was meant for me. I'm going to look elsewhere, Penny."

"You're giving up? Well I never. Personally, I think you two want your heads banging together. You're potty about each other and you're allowing a little thing like this to break it up."

"A little thing?" Adam shook his head. He had thought at the least that Penny understood but it seemed not. "Climbing means a lot to me. I thought you'd know that." He smiled a little, accepting the sympathy etched in Penny's face, in her whole manner. "I can't give it up."

"Why don't you get away for a while? It'll do you good, let you think things over. Only you can decide how much Catti means to you."

He wanted to say that Catherine meant everything to him, that she was the most important thing in his life, but he did not. He was beginning to regret involving Penny in his problems. It wasn't fair on her. She was right. Only he could decide.

"I might do that," he said thoughtfully. "Someone I know has been pestering me to tackle this climb with him. First, I said I would, then for various reasons, I backed out. But now ... I do believe I'll take him up on it. It sounds interesting. Modest rock face with a small overhang. A two-man job. He's not the man I would normally have chosen to climb with but I need all the practice I can get. Once I get up there, then I can clear my mind and let myself think. It's a helluva way of putting things in perspective."

"I'm sure it is," Penny said brightly. "I understand but I'm not so sure Catti will. Perhaps it will be better if I tell her you've gone off to some quiet retreat to think things over ... if she asks that is," she added quietly.

"Thanks." Adam resisted a sudden overwhelming impulse to dash out and drive over to see her. All he wanted to do was to take her in his arms and convince her once and for all what she meant to him. But it wasn't going to be that easy. Catherine was still bruised and battered from the shock of losing Joe. She still had to be treated with infinite care. "And for God's sake don't mention who I'm going with," he added hastily. "I particularly don't want her to know that."

"No, of course not. Who are you going with?" Penny asked, sitting in a blaze of innocence.

Adam laughed. "No one you know. Just an acquaintance of mine. Now ..." he smiled brightly. "How about a sweet?"

"Oh please. Something dreadfully creamy, I think." Penny consulted the menu. "An acquaintance? Not a friend? I'm sorry, I didn't catch his name."

The sand was moist and heavy, taking a long time to dry out. Catti squelched her way to a drier patch, taking her shoes off and slapping them free of the clinging grains of sand.

It was good to be alone. She understood what people meant when they wanted to be alone. She was still astonished that she had put the phone down on him. Twice. She had not slammed it down, merely replaced it with measured care, patting it gently as the connection was severed. She loved him but she would have to let him go. There was no alternative. It was a waste of time trying to explain the logic to anyone. No one understood. Not even Penny, who understood most things.

If, as Suzanne suggested, it was just another casual affair for him, then it would not matter. He would get over it. He might be over it already.

She loved Adam more than he loved her. Simple. Just as Joe had loved her more than she had loved him. Equally simple.

She took a deep, steadying breath, closing her eyes, smelling the sea, the sand, hearing the gulls, the lapping water close by. Opening her eyes, she viewed things mistily. The sea was grey-brown today, shimmering to a blue-green distance as the sun edged out of a frothy cloud. It was very beautiful, calm and restful. And also comforting.

Spinning round, she could see Bay's End, wide-awake and attentive, as coolly grey as the water. She had to renew her fight for it. She wanted Adam far, far way. They could not possibly be just friends. She had only to look at him to remember.

Pulling her jacket closer, she walked back to the shore. Penny wanted to see her. She knew why. Penny had been meeting up with Adam and, presumably, Penny was going to try to persuade her that all was well. Penny could talk to her until she was blue in the face but that central issue would remain. All he had to do was give up the climbing. That was all she was asking. That was all. Just that.

"Quiet, Bobby, it's only Catti." Penny shooed the dog back to his basket and smiled a welcome. "You look cold. Have you been walking on the beach in this weather? You'll catch your death. And I bet you haven't got a thermal vest on either?"

Catti smiled. "Shut up, Penny. I'm not one of your girls. If I want to freeze, I'll freeze. Have you noticed the sea today? It's an extraordinary colour."

"Can't say I have. It just looks like the sea to me. Its usual murky winter colour." She gave Catti a sideways glance. "But then I'm not an artist. You must look at life through a different pair of eyes."

Catti sat on an old armchair nearest the blazing coal fire, looking round the room with some pleasure. Lived in. She loved Penny's house. She loved the cheerful family clutter. Last week's Sunday papers were still strewn around. A few battered dolls. A menagerie of plants. A blue budgie cheeping for all he was worth. And, from the kitchen, a delicious aroma.

"I've had lunch with that marvellous man of yours," Penny began confidently, moving some books so that she could sit down. "Isn't this piggy? Excuse it, won't you? I'm just trying out a new recipe and I've not got round to cleaning up yet. Wish I could afford a cleaning lady ..." she added, raising her eyebrows. "Now, where was I? Oh yes, that marvellous man of yours."

"He is not my marvellous man," Catti said. "And I resent the fact that's he's using you as his spokeswoman. If he's anything to say, why doesn't he say it himself?"

"Because you won't listen. You put the phone down on him, didn't you, so he assumed that you wouldn't listen. He's absolutely distraught, poor man." She flashed a glance at Catti. "I don't know what you're playing at but, if you don't watch it, you're going to lose him."

"His wife says they're getting back together," Catti said helplessly. "What do you expect me to do about that?"

"I've told you that's just not true. Good Lord, Catti, can't you tell when a man's sincere?"

"Maybe he is but...." She watched the dancing coals making patterns in the fire. She could see a figure there, Adam, hanging onto a slender piece of coal-black rock. Slipping. Flailing. Plummeting down. Lying in a crumpled, broken heap. The piece of coal ignited afresh, glowing, and suddenly she could no longer see him. It was just a piece of coal. Her imagination was on high alert.

"He's talking of backing out of Bay's End," Penny said quietly. "You're not going to let him do that surely?"

"It'll save me a lot of bother, won't it? Perhaps it will be better all round if he does that. Where is he anyway?" she asked, firing the question so unexpectedly that Penny immediately looked guilty.

"I don't know," she said. "No idea."

Catti looked at her carefully. "Penny ..." she said warningly.

"Oh all right then, although I promised I wouldn't tell. He's gone to one of those country retreats, a sort of monastery existence, living off bread and water. It'll give him the chance to contemplate. Don't ask me where it is. Northumberland, I think...."

Catti could not help a little smile. "You liar," she said. "Tell me where he's gone, Penny. Please."

"Why? I'm not telling you unless something positive's going to come out of it. For once in my life, I'm going to keep a confidence. He doesn't want you to know. Leave him, Catti."

"He's gone off climbing, hasn't he?" Catti asked, Penny's expression instantly confirming her fears. "That's why you're trying to protect him." She clicked her tongue in exasperation. "Wouldn't you know it? The first thing he thinks of when there's a problem is to go climbing. He's just like Joe. He just won't learn."

"And the first thing you do when there's a problem is paint," Penny reminded her amiably. "Same thing when you get down to it."

"It is *not* the same thing and you know it. I'm not going to have a fatal accident when I'm painting, am I? Will you please tell me where he's gone?"

"No." Penny stuck out her chin defiantly. "No, I will not. I've no sympathy with you this time. You don't give men like Adam and Don ultimatums. It's not fair."

"Why isn't it?" Catti demanded. Something, somewhere, told her she was wrong and Penny was right. This was like swimming through quicksands. She couldn't get out of it. She was too deeply stuck in a whirl of emotion.

"If Joe had listened to me, he'd still be here."

"Oh, there's no talking to you," Penny said crossly. "You want everything so cosy and safe. Life's not like that. Hasn't it occurred to you that he could make you this promise and promptly go out and be knocked down by a bus? There are no guarantees."

"Don't start that old argument," Catti said, suddenly tired. It was time to change the subject as Penny was obviously not going to tell her where Adam had gone. "Where did you put the painting?" she asked brightly.

"Oh yes. In the dining-room. We've just finished redecorating. Come and have a look."

The dining-room was neat as a pin, a startling contrast to the other room. A spring theme with pale green walls and floral curtains. The smell of paint lingered but the window was tightly closed against the grey of the day. "Like it?" Penny asked proudly. "Isn't it lovely? And look at your painting. Doesn't it look absolutely super on that wall?"

Catti smiled. Pleased. For a moment, she had eyes only for the painting in its new home. She had decided to give it to Penny on impulse, realizing that it reminded her too much of Adam. She gazed silently at it now, remembering that day by the lake.

"I'll leave you a while," Penny said softly at her side, showing a delicacy she did not normally possess. "I'll go and put the kettle on."

It was an awesome painting, very striking, not pretty, in no way pretty. A powerful, simmering cauldron of a painting. She surveyed it for some time. Yes ... she was proud of it.

"You can have it back if you like," Penny said, reappearing so suddenly that Catti turned round, startled. "I don't know why you gave it to me but, if you've changed your mind, do take it back. Don thinks it's far too expensive a present anyway. You know very well we can't possibly afford your prices."

"No, it's yours," Catti insisted. "Now ... we've just one thing to clear up before I go."

"What's that?" Penny looked at her suspiciously. "You're not still expecting me to tell you, are you? I promised I wouldn't."

Catti sighed. "Penny, we've known each other a long time. Don't do this to me."

Penny frowned down, picking at a loose thread on her open-wave sweater, avoiding Catti's accusing look. "If you suddenly turn up, he'll know it's me who's told you. I hate having this reputation of not being able to keep a secret."

"I just want to talk to him." Catti followed her back into the sitting-room where tea was waiting. "I can see now that Suzanne was making a fool of me. And I fell for it. I could kick myself for that. I just sat there and let her say all those things about Adam. None of it was true."

"She's clever." Penny was still trying to repair the damage she had done to her sweater. "The fact that she's on television doesn't help. It's that candid look to camera. How can anyone fail to believe her? Don would believe her if she said the moon was made of green cheese. I might well have been taken in by her myself."

No. Penny would not. Nevertheless, Catti was grateful to her. At least it made her own reaction seem a little less naive.

"Do you love him, Catti?"

Catti felt herself flush. She could not say it. All she could do was nod her head slightly and look away.

"And I've talked to him. He's mad about you, Catti. I'm sure you can work it out between you. You've got to or you're going to regret it for the rest of your lives." She gave a little contented smile. "I want you to be as happy as we are. Oh, I know we have our ups and downs and I grumble like hell about him but honestly...." She seemed to come to a sudden decision, straightening her body in the chair. "All right, I will tell you. At least, I'll tell you as much as I know. I don't know exactly where he's staying but you can ring round the hotels and guest-houses and find out. He's going on this climb, practice stuff, a two-man climb. With somebody called ... oh no, he didn't want you to know who he'd gone with...."

"Penny, for goodness sake, will you stop twittering around and tell me," Catti said, hardly daring to breathe in case Penny had second thoughts.

"Somebody called Eric somebody...."

"What?" Catti's limbs turned to jelly. She was glad she was already sitting down or she knew she would have collapsed. Not only was he off climbing but he was off with Eric. Why, was beyond her. Eric, who was not an experienced climber, who took too many risks, and hadn't Eric every reason to dislike Adam after all that had happened at the wedding?

"What's the matter? Do you know him?"

"Where are they?"

"Hold your horses, I'm just coming to that." She bit her lip anxiously.

Catti listened with a deepening despair. She remembered the look Eric had given Adam when he had left them in the Garden Room that night. If looks could kill....

And Adam would be putting his trust in a man like that. Roped together.

She had to find him. She had to stop him.

Would she be in time?

Thirteen

She kept remembering the dream with worrying clarity. Eric was there, grinning. He held a knife in his hands and he was cutting through the rope that bound him to Adam. Adam was powerless to stop him, swinging helplessly against the rock. Below them, space.

She told herself to calm down. Whatever else Eric might be, he was not a cold-blooded murderer. But he was careless and that was not a comfortable thought. She knew from things Joe had said that there was no room for carelessness in a team.

Catti felt suffocated by feelings of guilt. She ought never to have hung up on him. That was the coward's way out and she had things to tell him. It was important that she see him, face to face, that she was honest with him at last, that she told him of her very real fears.

She tried the Tweed hotel in that area first but had no luck. Then she began to work her way through the smaller hotels and guest-houses. Grace appeared with a cup of tea halfway through and gave her an encouraging smile. Even so, it was her ninth or tenth attempt before she found him. The voice, bright and female, from Mere View Guest House confirmed that a Mr Adam Trent was registered with them but that he was out at the moment. "Would you hold the line, please? Ah yes ... Mrs Trent is here if you wish to speak with her. I'll ask her to come to the telephone."

"No ..." Catti struggled with a reply, shocked by the news that Suzanne was with him. "No thank you, it's not important. I'll call back."

"Would you care to leave a message, madam?"

Madam most certainly would not. Not with Suzanne. What was she up to?

As she replaced the receiver, a sudden heavy sadness pressed down on her, coupled with a deadening disappointment. So much for Penny's assurance that Suzanne had been bluffing. According to Penny, there was as much chance of a reconciliation between Adam and Suzanne as there was of she and Don getting a divorce.

She had so wanted it to be true but it obviously was not. Suzanne was not giving him up easily. But ... neither was she. Impatiently, Catti tossed aside the disappointment, replacing it with a cold, calculated resolve. If she believed anything Adam had told her during that wonderful night they had spent together then she had to give him another chance. To hell with what people might think! She would be baring her soul for who but a woman in love would set off on a wild-goose chase with no guarantee of a successful outcome?

"Any luck?" Grace popped her head round the door. "Found him yet?"

After the briefest hesitation, Catti told her. "Is there any point in me going?" she asked, anxious for reassurance even though she had already made up her mind. "How can I possibly compete with a woman like her?"

"He's left her once," Grace said thoughtfully. "Something went wrong, didn't it? But she won't let him go. I know a few people like that. Now, the way I see it is this ..." she paused, frowning. "You've agreed to marry him if he hangs up his climbing boots...?"

Catti nodded. "That's about the gist of it, Grace. Sounds simple put like that."

"Take my Jimmy ... when I first met him, dear, he was mad about fishing. Sit for hours on a damp riverbank just staring into the water. Hours, dear. I couldn't see the sense of it myself and I told him as much. I went with him once and I was bored to death after about ten minutes."

They exchanged a sympathetic, female smile. "Mad, I said to him; if you think I'm going to sit here with you week after week, you can forget it." She nodded with some satisfaction. "Gave it to him straight, I did. We were married shortly afterwards. Sell your fishing rods, I said to him, the money will come in useful."

"And did he?"

"Oh no." Grace looked puzzled. "Don't you see what I'm getting at? Compromise, that's what you have to do."

"That doesn't sound like compromise, that sounds like giving in," Catti said.

"What if he wanted you to give up your painting?"

"That's different. I couldn't possibly give up painting. It's very special to me, Grace, it's...." She stopped, willing Grace to understand.

"And that's how he feels, dear, about his climbing," Grace said, starting work with a vengeance, wielding the broom with cheerful abandon.

Recognizing her embarrassment, Catti decided not to pursue the matter further. She thought she understood what Grace was trying to tell her. In simple words, she had to do what she wanted, deep down, and to hell with all this useless agonizing. "I'm going to pack a bag," she said decisively. "Then I'll be off. It won't take long."

Grace made absolutely no comment on Catti's plans, bursting instead into song, as she was fond of doing. Catti smiled as she tidied up her brushes. Somehow the choice, a particularly evocative romantic ballad, seemed entirely appropriate.

For someone as rusty as he was, it was not an easy climb and Adam had to acknowledge that halfway through. He had lost his footing and if it hadn't been for Eric up there.... With a final supreme effort, he hoisted himself over the ledge and pulled himself clear, breathing hard. He gulped great gasps of the cool, sweetly fresh air. City lungs would be shocked by this, he thought, still gulping, before subsiding thankfully beside Eric on flat coarse grass. God, that had been exhausting. Exhilarating. Exquisite.

He grasped Eric's hand firmly. "Thanks," he said simply. No need to say anything else. Below them, the rock face fell steeply, dizzily away. Above them, they had yet more rock to negotiate before they reached the top but the worst was now over. Plenty of easy handholds from now on, very nearly a doddle.

"Bloody good eh? Glad you came?" Eric was still catching his breath, not quite in peak condition. "Look at that view!"

Picture postcard stuff. Spread before them like a pretty jigsaw. A warm day. The cold snap over, could it be that this was the first hint of spring? *This* was what it was all about. *This* was what you could not explain to people who did not care. And he was damned lucky. Not everyone had the chance to see life from this angle. He had been scared back there. He didn't mind admitting it. Roped. Secure. But, for a moment, as he grappled for his footing, he had felt fear grip him in its cold vice. And that was what it was all about too. Testing yourself to the limits of your capability and coming through. How could he explain to Catherine?

He had made up his mind to go to the Himalayas this summer and not even Catherine was going to stop him. It was something he had to do.

They were silent, absorbed in their own thoughts. Eric stirred at last, sitting up and rubbing his thickly stockinged legs.

"Sorry about that business at the wedding," he said quietly. "Misjudgement. It won't happen again." He glanced sharply at Adam, a wicked look in his eye. "Have you got something going with her?" he asked. "Lucky devil."

"I'm going to marry her," Adam said. "Once we've got one or two things sorted out."

"Oh...." Eric hid his surprise. "Congratulations. No hard feelings?"

He held out his hand once more. Adam took it.

"He's still out, madam." Mrs Gloria Wilson, the proprietor of Mere View Guest House, the owner of the bright, shrill voice, beamed. She was a very large lady, in pale lilac, not young but with a beautiful clear skin and a crisp laundered look enhanced by discreet jewellery. "If you'd like to go through to the lounge, you're just in time for afternoon tea. Home-made fruit cake, almond biscuits and a pot of tea? That all right? Mrs Trent's in there, I do believe. Sitting there quietly all afternoon. Reading, I think. She's a very quiet lady. Very genteel, you know."

"I...." Even as Catti debated how to get out of this, Mrs Wilson was majestically sailing down a corridor, already opening a white-panelled door marked "Visitors' Lounge". She peered into the gloom, ahead of Catti, before applying her fingers to a mass of light switches just inside. "Sitting in the dark, Mrs Trent?" she enquired with a laugh. "I have a visitor for you and then I'll bring you tea. Home-made fruit cake, almond biscuits and a pot of tea? That all right?"

Catti remained standing just inside the door when Mrs Wilson had bustled off in search of tea. "I'm sorry," she said, her confusion making her stumble over the words. "I thought ... that is ... are you Mrs Trent? I was expecting to see ... oh how silly of me."

"I'm Adam's mother. Come in ... Catherine, isn't it?" She smiled a welcome, a slim lady with startling blue eyes, Adam's eyes, wearing a pink twin-set, tweed skirt and a double row of pearls. Catti edged in nervously, feeling ridiculously, annoyingly, about fifteen. "Adam's told me so much about you," Mrs Trent went on. "On the drive up. He talked of nothing else. It makes me feel that I know you already."

They shook hands a little shyly. "It's lovely to meet you," Catti said. "Where is he? Mrs Wilson doesn't seem to know."

"They've gone off climbing." She pointed vaguely over her shoulder. "That dark pointy hill, you know the one I mean. Adam didn't think it would take very long." She rearranged the pearls. "I was actually enjoying sitting here in the twilight. Thinking. I often sit and think at home without realizing that I'm in the dark. Bright lights are just a confusion."

There was a short companiable silence as their afternoon tea arrived, fussily accompanied by Mrs Wilson herself. "I didn't intend to come along this week-end," Mrs Trent remarked when they were alone once more. "It was a complete surprise. Adam came along and said pack your bag I'm taking you to the Lakes. He can be like that. So impulsive. And thoughtful." Her smile was proud, motherly. "He and Suzanne ..." she paused, fingering the pearls, "I do hope you don't mind me saying this and I shan't mention her name ever again but ... he and Suzanne were never right for each other. Mothers know these things. I knew instantly when you appeared out of the gloom," she smiled impishly. "I knew at once that you and Adam would make a first-class team."

Catti smiled at the old-fashioned phrase. "I know that," she said quietly. "But I'm glad you think so too."

"You want him to give up climbing?" It was a direct question requiring a direct answer. Nothing less would do.

"It's been hard," Catti began thoughtfully, assessing her own reaction even as she spoke. "Yesterday, I would have said yes. But today...." She shrugged. "Something somebody said. Something about compromise."

Mrs Trent poured the tea. "Welcome to the family, my dear," she said.

Adam and Eric were late back. Mrs Wilson tried to remain composed even though it played havoc with her supper schedule. She had placed them at a table for four in the corner by the fire. Dinner for four with Mrs Trent looking serene and Eric looking uncomfortable.

They skirted round the real reason for Catti being here. Although she sensed Adam's reservations, Eric could not be stopped and chatted non-stop about the climb they had done, dwelling on the more hair-raising moments, stopping short as he realized Catti was sitting beside him, suddenly conscious he might have touched a raw nerve.

"Mr Chambers ..." Mrs Trent smiled her very pretty smile. "I want to know all about your exploits. You and I will retire and have our coffee in the lounge. If you'll excuse us...."

"Sorry about Eric being here," Adam apologized at once. His smile was shaky. "I didn't know you were coming over.... Penny told you where I was, I suppose?"

"Only after practically being stretched on the rack," Catti assured him. "I had to talk to you, Adam, to explain things." She smiled helplessly, finding it difficult to say what she wanted to say now that they were alone, or almost alone.

"You don't have to explain anything," he said. "I...." He broke off as Mrs Wilson appeared at their side, not very happy that two of their party had sneaked off before dessert. Somewhat aggressively, she rhymed off a tempting list of home-made sweets. Thus intimidated, they ordered.

"If she says home-made once more...." Adam smiled and she blessed him for trying to make it easier for her. "I saw your painting up at Penny's house," he continued quietly, his mood changing. "It took me back to that day we spent by the lake. Turned out all wrong, didn't it? The painting was fantastic."

"Did you like it?" Again she felt that ridiculous pleasure at his praise.

"I liked it." A smile was playing round his lips, his eyes were amused too, his skin flushed from the day in the open air and the proximity now to the blazing fire. "Catherine...?" He whispered her name, reaching across the table to touch her hand, a feathery brushing of his fingers against hers, a touch so fragile that it made her catch her breath, made her eyes sparkle their delight, made her lips part. "I've missed you so much, my love," he said.

Her heart thudded. An overwhelming cloud of emotion, of love for him, spun dizzily all around. It took a moment to recover her poise.

"This afternoon ... on the rock face ... I thought about you," he said softly. "I hate the thought of you sitting worrying about me when I'm up there."

"But...?" she prompted gently. "Say it, Adam. You can't give it up, can you?"

There was a silence and then he shook his head. "No. I can't," he said. "I'm sorry, Catherine."

And she couldn't give him up either. Looking at him, his face partly in shadow from a nearby lamp, she knew she would take the risk. He was worth it. "We'll have to fix a date," she said brightly, enjoying his start of surprise. "How about spring? Then we'll have time for a honeymoon before you go off with Stuart. And I've got to get my paintings organized for the exhibition so I'll be kept busy whilst you're in the Himalayas."

She knew exactly what he was just about to say, what

he would have said, if Mrs Wilson hadn't suddenly and quite silently appeared holding aloft plates of a steaming ginger pudding.

So ... for the moment it remained unsaid and they exchanged a smile instead, a secret lovers' smile. And *that* said it all.